THE BUSINESS
OF DYING

THE BUSINESS OF DYING

THE COMPLETE WESTERN STORIES

RICHARD S. WHEELER

BLACK STONE PUBLISHING

Printed in the United States of America

ISBN 978-1-5047-8879-3
Fiction / Westerns

1 3 5 7 9 10 8 6 4 2

CIP data for this book is available from the Library of Congress

Blackstone Publishing
31 Mistletoe Rd.
Ashland, OR 97520
www.BlackstonePublishing.com

CONTENTS

FOREWORD

Long ago, I spent several years in rural Arizona, near the Mexican border. I was between newspaper jobs, and hoped to make a living with free-lance writing. I soon discovered that the remote border area was populated by various eccentric and gaudy people, who for various reasons chose to live as far as possible from civilization.

Some were notable. One had been Jack Dempsey's trainer. His wife had been a Ziegfeld Follies chorus girl. Another was a successful screenwriter, who kindly taught me how to write fiction. I owe my success to him. But most were simply people like me, looking for adventure in an obscure corner of the states.

They all had stories. One, a rancher, had roped a mountain lion and lived to tell about it. Johnny Carson even invited him to talk about it. I heard plenty of stories during my sojourn there, many of them told by the people who lived on a guest ranch that bordered Mexico. One of the stories included here involved a crazy attempt to graft a small piece of Mexican territory to the United States. I witnessed that one.

Eventually I returned to civilization, but the stories stayed with me. And an odd thing was happening. They kept getting funnier. Every time I told one of those stories, the event seemed more comic.

By the time I got to writing them down, a few years ago, the stories had turned into comedy. I fictionalized the actual characters and events, and in the process added to the comedy, but, even so, these stories were inherently funny, and that is how they appear here.

In addition to the contemporary stories, I wrote historical ones. These were based on the usual research, largely gotten from books. But some of those became comic too. The result is this anthology, which is mostly humor, some of it bizarre.

My favorite by far of the historical short stories is "The Square Reporter". It is about a real person, William Wright, a reporter for the *Territorial Enterprise* in Virginia City, Nevada. He was a friend of Samuel Clemens, who also wrote for the paper. They were fierce rivals when it came to publishing the wildest and most outlandish hoaxes they could dream up. Wright, whose pen name was Dan DeQuille, was a master at the game, and came up with what was probably the best hoax in the history of journalism.

DeQuille's story was about an inventive sort who intended to cross Death Valley in the heat of summer, wearing a suit of armor that would protect him from the deadly sun. The armor would contain a thick layer of sponge, which would hold enough water to keep him cool, and get him across the lethal valley. In that story — get this! — the traveler freezes to death because the evaporation from the sponges cooled him too fast. It was widely reprinted and believed in reputable London papers and around the globe, while the news people in Nevada were enjoying the hoax.

In my own story about William Wright, one of the major mining entrepreneurs, Jim Fair asks him to descend into his sealed-off mine and observe what might be the biggest bonanza in the history of the Comstock Lode. Which he does. And you will find the result of all that within.

Richard S. Wheeler

MUGS BIRDSONG'S CRIME ACADEMY

I

They handed Mugs Birdsong two dollars and stuffed him into a cheap gray suit, and escorted him to the gate of the Wyoming State Penitentiary that fine spring day.

The warden, L.L. Grubbenheider, was beaming. "We'll be seeing ya, Mugs," he said, offering the evicted con a hearty handshake.

He knew what he was talking about. Mugs was the most famous criminal in the country. He was known from coast to coast. From Mexico to Canada. There was no crime he hadn't attempted, and no crime he wouldn't try. Mothers warned their daughters that when Mugs Birdsong was loose in the world, nothing was safe. Fathers warned their sons that they should not admire Mugs Birdsong, even though there were ballads written about him, and he had replaced Billy the Kid as the most celebrated crook in the universe.

Mugs had gotten off easy this time, serving only five years. He was still a young man, in his forties, with a life ahead of him. He rarely was in prison for long. His technique was to stare at the juries, mesmerizing them, awakening terror in them, so they all returned verdicts he could live with. More than one juror reported that he feared for his life, the way Mugs was staring at him during the trial. Other jurors routinely begged judges to be excused from jury duty whenever there was a Mugs Birdsong trial.

But the warden was correct. He'd be seeing Mugs again, probably sooner rather than later. Mugs didn't mind, either way. The pen at Rawlins was a noble and hospitable establishment, and life was just as fine inside as out. It was run by the Wyoming Board of Charities and Reform, which suited Mugs just fine. They had worked mightily at reforming him, and he had enjoyed it. But now he stood on the steps, not so much a free man as one who had the annoying task of providing a living for himself. Two dollars would not last long. Being free was sometimes a pain in the ass.

The air was chill, and his sleazy suit did not turn the cold. He stepped down to the road and wandered into a raw high-plains town that had no excuse to exist. Mostly it fed local ranchers and housed prison guards and was a whistle stop. Mugs Birdsong was on the loose, and dogs slinked away, tail between their legs, and shivering wives locked their front doors, and children stared from behind lilac bushes. The marvelous thing about Mugs was that he stole from the poor and gave to the rich.

Mugs liked the town. No one in his right mind wanted to live in Rawlins, which is why the town was juicy and pleasant to Mugs. He debated what to do. Two dollars wouldn't take him far, but that was no problem. It wouldn't buy him much hamburger, but that was no problem. Whatever he needed he took, so there never was a problem in all of his life. He had taken fortunes from quivering financiers, and candy from babies. In all his life, Mugs Birdsong had never had a problem clothing, feeding, or sheltering himself. Neither had he ever had a problem finding a mate. He simply took whatever was convenient, and that resolved the matter. He had made several ladies very happy, and one or two very sad.

He stopped in at the local beanery, and the counter boy recognized him instantly, set a bowl of chili before the renowned criminal with trembling hand, and refused pay for it. That's how it was with Mugs. He never had any problems with life.

He eyed the sleepy burg, looking for a saloon. It had been years since he had wet his whistle, and a foaming mug seemed a fine idea. Down the street, the Parsnip Saloon announced itself, so Mugs ambled that direction, entered through a double door, and found himself in a dank and gloomy interior that exuded strange odors. The pen was a better place. In the dim light he discovered a barkeep with a soiled apron and an arm garter.

"A mug of cold beer, that's what I need," Mugs said.

"Show me your dime first," the keep said.

Mugs laughed. "I got a two-dollar going-away present right here, pal, and that buys a lot of suds."

The keep looked him over. "For you it's free. I don't want no trouble." He drew a mug, let the foam settle, and filled it brim full.

Mugs grinned. "It'll do, and the next one's on you, too."

"Like you say," the keep said, and retreated.

"Hey! Come talk to me. I'm twenty minutes a free man and no one wants my company."

"I didn't mean to offend, sir," the keep said.

"Well, you did, so you can buy me a few more mugs after this."

"You're a famous man, sir. I'm honored to have you step inside this poor excuse for a saloon."

Damn, it was enjoyable. Mugs felt like a vaudeville star. He felt like a candidate for high office. He felt like the pope. He sipped his suds while the keep smiled and wiped the bar with a sticky cloth and adjusted the shutters, letting in some light. Maybe he wanted Rawlins' citizens to see what he had on a bar stool.

After a while the keep ventured a little closer.

"Sam Bearmouth here...I guess I know your moniker."

"I guess you do, and you're still alive to tell about it," Mugs said.

"Yeah, you're the king of all crime, all right. You mind if I let people know you're here? I'd sell a few beers."

"Go right ahead, Sam. You can give me a fifty-fifty cut."

"Yeah, well, I'll do that. You mind if I leave you here a little? I got to spread the word."

"Up to you," Mugs said. "Are you insured? I could do a little arson."

"No...I mean, I don't need that. I need cash."

"Well, you go spread the word, and leave the cash drawer open, and I'll split what you've got with you."

"Ah, I think I'll stick around."

"Word's out, you know. I held up the beanery."

"You held it up? Ten minutes after getting out?"

"Figure of speech, Sam. But they were pleased to give me a free feed and stay alive. It's a miracle. I walk in and they all treat me like visiting royalty."

"Well, staying alive's the thing," Sam said. He peered around sorrowfully. "Nobody knows you're in here. Maybe you could step out and spread the word?"

"Sure, if you hand me what's in your cash drawer. I never do nothing for free."

Sam looked mighty sorrowful. He saw his big opportunity sliding away.

"Here you are, the kingpin of all crime, and it's just you and me in here. Do you think we could get a reporter in? It'd make my place famous. I know just the man, Willis Wilcox, from the weekly here. He'd do a fine story."

"Reporters all wet their pants writing me up," Mugs said. "I don't like reporters."

"Well, how about me getting a photographer? Nice photo, you and me, hanging on the wall and I'd be a rich man. Everyone in three counties would be in for a look-see."

"Hey, I'm so ugly I'd break the lens, Sam. But if he wants to pay me a hunnert, I'd pocket it and let him. And for a hunnert from you, I'll stand next to you with a hand around your shoulder, like we're partners in crime."

"You'd do that...for me?"

"Sure, but don't try to whittle down the price. I name a price and it's do or die."

Sam applied his gummy rag to the bar, and thought about that. "Nah, I think I'll pass on that. I'd have to go to the Stockmen's Bank for a loan."

Mugs slid his beer stein toward the keep, who promptly filled it, taking care to drain off the foam. "Here," Sam said. "Say, how about an autograph? You famous and all? I've got a napkin you can write on."

"How do I spell Mugs?" Birdsong said. "I can never figure it out."

"I give up," Sam said. "You defeat me."

"I'm just a regular hood," Mugs said.

"No, you're not. You're genius. You should start a crime school."

"That touches my fancy, Sam. Sometimes you're a good barkeep."

Heartened, Sam plunged onward. "Yeah, a crime college. The finest in the country. A place to get a doctoral degree in crime, like those professors."

"I always knew I liked you," Mugs said.

"I mean, if you're going to get taught, get taught right, right?"

"You can pour more suds, Sammy, my boy."

The barkeep did as directed, deposited the mug before Mugs, and then waxed eloquent. "I bet you'd have students from all over the country...Mugs Birdsong's College of Crime. You'd show 'em how it's done, right?"

"Sammy, boy, you're inspiring me," Mugs said. "A crime college. Advanced degrees in crime. A master's degree in crime, from Mugs Birdsong. Something to hang on the wall, right?"

"Righto," Sam agreed.

"Now this here university, who's gonna come, and who's gonna pay?"

"Why, half the peace officers in the country. And their counties and states would pay the freight."

"Sammy, you inspire me. For that you can pour me another. I have acquired a thirst after five years in the bosom of the local hospitality house."

Sammy filled another mug, seeing as how Mugs hadn't drained the first one.

"Now, Sammy, boy, how would I start this college?"

"Oh, that's easy. There's an abandoned orphanage over in Rock Springs. You go there and announce it, and see who shows up."

"An abandoned orphanage?"

"Yeah, these days they haul the little turds out to the ranches and sell them off. They make good workers. The Orphan Train from back east started it."

"And what would I teach at my University of Crime?"

"Train robbery one-oh-one, bank robbery one-oh-one, with advanced courses later. Kidnapping and ransom studies. Bribing judges seminar. Gang warfare. You name it, you can teach it."

"Pour me another, Sam. This is a fruitful morning. How am I gonna advertise this establishment?"

"Your name will do it, sir. The Mugs Birdsong University, or the Mugs Birdsong Institute of Advanced Criminology."

"And what would I teach?"

"How to do it."

"How do I get this orphanage?"

Sam shrugged. "Just take it."

That intrigued Mugs. He'd never stolen an orphanage before. The prospect pleased him. He thought he'd head for Rock Springs and steal the orphanage and start his college of crime. He thought he might need some trappings. Like a bank to rob, and a railway express car, and a few things like that, but Rock Springs would be glad to have the new business, and would lend him whatever he needed. There were rails running through town; he could get the railroads to give him an express car, or baggage car, and a locomotive. There were things to teach about locomotives. Like how to keep the engineer from blowing the whistle to summon help. Yes, Rock Springs might just be the place for the king of crime to settle, and teach the world what he knew.

"Sammy, my boy, I'm heading for Rock Springs. You tell your customers that you're the one put the College of Crime in Mugs Birdsong's head, and you'll have a whole mess of altar boys in here."

"Glad to do ya a favor, Mugs," Sam said.

"Yeah, one last thing, Sam. Come to the station and buy me a ticket."

II

Mugs Birdsong didn't think much of Rock Springs. The people were mean, unlike the people in Rawlins. Rock Springs was surrounded by parched slopes that were ugly to look at, which made people ornery. He found the old orphanage without trouble; it sat next to the railroad tracks, so orphans could be shipped here and there.

It was pretty tumble-down, but maybe he could get the sheriff's road gang to smooth it up. Some windows were broken. Other than that, it looked like a good deal. There were about twenty rooms, a kitchen and dining room, and three classrooms. His college could house about twenty peace officers at a time, feed them and teach them, and send them back to their districts well-schooled in every known branch of crime, and taught by the king of criminals himself.

Who said that crime wouldn't pay?

He circled the decaying building a time or two, tried the door, and headed for the sheriff, Barney Stoopnagle. He'd never met the sheriff, but they were old buddies, sharing space on Wanted posters. Mugs was above, Stoopnagle at the bottom of each sheet. He found the sheriff in Rocky Dell Eatery, enjoying a breakfast tamale.

"Well, well, well," said Stoopnagle.

"I like tamales...want to share?" Mugs asked, sliding onto the seat next to the sheriff.

A miraculous thing happened. Stoopnagle shoved the half-eaten tamale toward Mugs.

"Don't mind if I do," Mugs said, wolfing the loot. "My mother's grandmother was from Vera Cruz. We have tamales in the family tree."

"What brings you to Rock Springs?" the sheriff asked, wiping his mouth with his sleeve.

"I'm going to start an academy of crime. The latest and best crime techniques. It'll be a draw, Sheriff."

"You don't say," the sheriff responded, for lack of anything better to say.

"In the old orphanage," Mugs added. "It's perfect."

"Is that so?" the sheriff said.

"I haven't chosen a name yet. But it will be devoted to higher education, and offer advanced degrees. Like masters degrees in liberal theft. Maybe you can help me choose a name for it."

"I'm faster with a gun," Stoopnagle said, bowing out.

"Then be a judge while I toss a few your way. How about The Mugs Birdsong Academy of Criminal Arts?"

"It has possibilities, Mugs."

"The Mugs Birdsong School of Felony?"

"Nah, that doesn't have a ring to it."

"The Rock Springs University of Crime?"

"Now you're cooking, Mugs. Say, you mind showing me your Rawlins release?"

"Look at my suit, dummy."

Stoopnagle eyed the wrinkled gray suit. "That'll do," he said.

"Now, have I got work for you, Sheriff. We've got to stage some train robberies and a few bank heists, so peace officers know how it's done. You'll need to roll an express car or baggage car in here, and put it on a siding, so we can stage some heists. And I want you to talk to the bank, so we can stage some heists there. I've gotta teach those students how it's done. And we'll need volunteers for kidnapping. Line up a few pretty little girls, or a banker or an alderman."

Mysteriously, the counter lady laid a whole platter of pancakes before the sheriff, and he was soon digging into them and adding syrup. He was one of the pancake eaters who never had enough sweet on top of the cakes. Mugs found a fork and snipped away a corner, and then a third before Stoopnagle got to it.

"Glad you agree with me," Mugs said.

Stoopnagle looked puzzled.

"I never refuse pancakes," Mugs said. "You know where the best cakes are? In the pen. We had a great kitchen in Rawlins. I'm going to put a great kitchen into the school. That orphanage looks like it has a dandy."

"You got that thing leased, Mugs?"

"I've got her nailed down and hog-tied," Mugs said. "Now, I want a steam engine, an express car, and a caboose. Sometimes cabooses work best. Jump a caboose, hog-tie the brakemen, walk the cars to the tender and engine, and aim at the fireman and engineer. Surprise, surprise!"

"I don't have much pull with the railroad, Mugs."

"That's all right. We'll get what we need. I have never lacked anything in all my days. Now, here's what you do...you pull some jailbirds into a gang, and you go polish up that old orphanage. I mean clean. That's going to be my university, and it's going to shine. I'm heading for the newspaper to announce the blessing."

"Blessing?"

"Rock Springs is about to become the Crime Capital of the World."

"I'm sure our people will be delighted, Mugs."

"Good! And don't let anyone interfere with the clean-up."

Mugs stabbed the last piece of pancake, and left. Pretty soon the old orphanage would shine. He was content. Life was perfect. He located *The Rock Springs Tattler* just off the business district, where the rent was cheaper.

The editor proved to be a gray-haired woman, which might slow things down slightly.

"You're beautiful," he said.

"You still pay for all printing and advertising," she said.

"I'm Mugs Birdsong. I think you ran some Wanted posters on me."

"I can't imagine anyone wanting you," she said.

"I have a story for your paper."

"It better be good," she said, "or out you go."

"I've taken over the orphanage. I'm starting the Mugs Birdsong College of Crime. Rock Springs will soon be the Crime Capital of the World."

"It already is, Mugs baby."

"No, not yet. We'll have courses on assaulting women, purse snatching, mugging, bigamy, harem slavery, suicide, and the Mann Act."

"You'll still have to pay for printing," she said.

"You put a notice in the paper, and print up an ad, and send it to lawmen across the country, two hundred dollars for a one-month crime doctorate degree, plus room and board."

"Pay in advance, sweetheart."

"Tonight or tomorrow night?"

She sighed sweetly. "You win, baby."

"I always pay my debts," he said. "Be ready. They call me Swifty. What did you say your name is?"

"Typhoid Mary, baby."

Mugs smiled, revealing the gap in his teeth where Jake Drink landed a long piece of lead pipe.

"Whistle while you work," he said, and exited.

Good! Another few tasks taken care of. It was such a fine day. Almost as good as being in the pen at Rawlins. The next step was some firearms. You couldn't teach a doctoral course in crime without a few weapons. He headed for the Bull Moose Brothers Hardware, hoping to find a fine selection in the display cases. He knew exactly what he wanted. A snub-nosed small revolver, a shotgun, and a sniper rifle. Sure enough, there was a fine display on hand. Rock Springs was a law-abiding and safe town, so everyone was armed to the teeth.

The proprietor hastened to the display case, eager to peddle his wares, but then he studied his customer and hesitated.

"I don't think so," he said.

"You are?"

"Mike Moose. No, sir, I have some scruples, you know. You're the face in every post office in the nation. How many felonies is it now?"

"I'd have to see the list, Moose baby. It reads like a Montgomery Ward catalog. A few hundred. Seven jail terms. Eighty-nine hung juries. Twelve murders that go unsolved. A hundred-nine deflowered ladies. I've cost several states a few hundred thousand smackeroos in legal and custody expenses. And that's all great news for Rock Springs. It's going to be the Crime Capital of the World, and you're going to like that. There'll be people coming in here to buy these fine weapons, and you'll hardly be able to keep them in stock. Now, I am looking for a garden-variety snub-nose, a shotgun, and a long-range rifle. They don't have to be fancy. All that stuff about having just the right weapon, the right balance, the right make, the right action, the right holster...that's just nothing but propaganda from hardware salesmen like you. The only thing that counts is reliability. Man, if it doesn't shoot, I'll come back here and shoot you."

"You don't frighten me a bit."

"It's for the Academy of Crime, bonehead. I need to teach my students how to employ each weapon. I'll have rooms full of lawmen eager to learn from me. You expect me to teach them using toys?"

"What academy of crime?"

"The Mugs Birdsong University of Crime, which will soon fill the old orphanage."

"You got references?"

"You send a wire to Rawlins, and they'll wire you straight up."

"How are you going to pay for these?"

"You're going to donate them to the university. Along with lots of blanks. We won't be using live ammo. Just a ton of blanks. It'll make your hardware store famous. Bull Moose Brothers Hardware has donated weapons and cartridges to the academy."

"I'll think about it, Birdsong."

"While you're thinking, I want to look at that snub-nose there under glass."

Mike Moose reluctantly drew a little .38 from the counter and handed it to Mugs. Mugs checked the action — nothing in the chambers — and pointed it straight at Moose.

"I'd be grateful if you'd point that somewhere else," Moose said.

"It's aimed straight at your cold heart. Mind if I try the action?"

Moose was growing oddly quivery. And his armpits grew rank.

"I'll take this and that double-barreled Browning shotgun, and that excellent Winchester there, and you can supply a box of cartridges or shells for each."

Moose seemed to melt into a puddle. The snub-nose never wavered. "You're robbing me," Moose whispered. "Broad daylight, too."

"Is this gun loaded?"

"Well, no, but robbing, that's what you're doing."

"How can I do that? It's not loaded. We both know that. I could pull the trigger all day long and you'd be standing there safe and sound."

"It's the...pressure you put on me, that's what."

"When you give me the guns, I'll write out a receipt. Then you'll feel better."

Moose stood there mesmerized. Then something sagged, and he lifted the shotgun and rifle off the racks and laid them on the glass counter top.

"Shells," Mugs said. "Lots of shells."

Sighing sadly, Moose found a box of them for the revolver, a box for the rifle, and started to look for shotgun shells.

"Double aught buckshot," Mugs said. "Twelve gauge."

Moose sighed and mumbled, and laid the box beside the others.

"Paper and nib?"

Moose slowly supplied these.

Mugs dipped the nib into the ink well and began scratching the receipt. It said:

One revolver, one shotgun, one rifle, paid in full, Mugs Birdsong Academy of Crime.

"Initial this," Mugs said. "Right there."

Moose slowly added his initials, sighing and moaning the whole time. Mugs took the receipt, stuffed it into the breast pocket of his sleazy suit, then added the snub-nose, and lifted the rifle, shotgun, and shells.

"Thanks, old pal. Rock Springs is gonna shine."

"I'm having a migraine," Mike Moose said. "I think I'll close up for the day."

"I'll be back," Mugs said. "The school's going to need lots of things."

III

Mugs Birdsong could not remember a day of his life when he was unhappy. He always had everything he ever wanted. The whole world was ripe fruit, waiting to be plucked. He couldn't understand people who were unhappy, and had concluded that something was wrong with them. How was it possible to be unhappy?

Now the academy was all coming together nicely. He still hadn't chosen a name, but maybe that was good. He might change the name from year to year, just to stay ahead of the tax collectors. But for the moment it would be the Mugs Birdsong Academy of Crime. He had an artisan, Marcus Boehm, build a gilded sign and mount it over the front door, and Mugs paid the artisan by protecting him from extortion.

"If anyone bothers ya, lemme know," he told Boehm. "He'll never bother ya again."

The flyers went out across the country, and pretty soon the reservations came in. There were plenty of lawmen who wanted to learn all about crime from the world's greatest expert. There were so many applications that Mugs hardly knew how to choose, so he arbitrarily selected twenty for the first term, because that was capacity, and stuffed the rest into the second and third terms. The fees piled up in the bank, and everyone was happy as could be. The academy was convenient. Lawmen needed only to board a transcontinental train, and step off at Rock Springs and walk a short distance to the academy.

But there were still loose ends. He could not teach the theory of bank robbery without a bank. Neither could he teach the theory of train robbery without an express car, and a whole train would work better, especially if one intended to rob passengers. But Mugs knew that he would soon have what he needed.

He headed for the Union Bank of Rock Springs, and found its president, J.J. Jones, ensconced in a gilded rear office that was barricaded by a comely secretary, Miss Opal Luster.

"Miss Luster, how you do shine this fine morning," he said. "I've come to discuss theater with J.J."

He knew that anyone with two Js in his name would be called J.J. And the last name would be forgotten.

"Opals don't shine, sir, they have luster."

"I'm a luster myself," he said. "But I want to lay some stuff on your boss. I'm the arch-criminal Mugs Birdsong, just released from confinement. You can tell by the suit. It's what they give you going out the door. I have some business with that gent in there. We'll discuss some theater, as I say."

She gave him a flirty smile. Some women just like crooks, and she was one. "Well, I'll go see," she said.

When she returned, she nodded blandly, and let him in.

"Well, well, well," said J.J. Jones. "I've been hearing about you."

"J.J., old pal, it's like a reunion. I've come to talk about robbing your bank."

"I hear you've reformed, Mugs."

"Reformed? Reformed? Are you trying to rob me of my manhood?"

"Well, I suppose you have a reputation to uphold," the banker said.

The man was as soft as chocolate mousse, but Mugs wouldn't let that bother him.

"You've heard about my Academy of Crime. In the orphanage.

We're getting cranked up for our first session. I've got twenty lawmen signed up, and if I don't flunk them, they'll have a master's degree in crime. I've got *The Tattler* printing up diplomas and a jail crew sweeping out the place."

"It sounds like a winner, Mugs."

"I'll be teaching all the details. They need to know how to do a heist, get it? By the time I'm done with them, they'll know everything I know, and be fully capable of the most horrendous crimes ever witnessed. Just look at my clippings if you doubt it. I've had the best press any criminal has ever seen in this republic."

"Makes sense, Mugs."

"J.J., we need a bank to rob, got it? It's theater. I'll show them how it's done. I'll show them where the horse holder should be, and what happens when a few hoods barge in here waving guns, and wanting your tellers to fill the sacks. Now, if this makes you nervous, you just lock up all your cash in the vault before we do the demonstration. You can even dismiss your tellers and we'll use actors, if I can find any. Actors are a worthless lot. But it'd be best to use actual tellers, wetting their pants when they see the muzzle of a big old revolver aiming at their tonsils."

"Well, Mugs, we'll be glad to help."

"I've signed up a mess of real fine sheriffs and all. A few old-timers and a few apprentices, this first time around. And I'm fishing for old Wyatt Earp and old Bat Masterson in the next session. Earp's up in Alaska running a saloon, and Masterson's writing horse-racing stuff in New York. He's getting a little wobbly on his pins, but he might be eager to learn, got it? I always say, go for the stars when you want to make a splash."

"Really? Legends of justice," Jones said. "I'd be honored to have such splendid men even walk into my humble little bank. Why, they're known from coast to coast."

"Yeah, J.J., we'll do one of these bank heists with each session. We'll also do a train robbery and a few other tidbits. Muggings, purse snatchings, extortion, white slavery, cruelty to animals, and so on. You don't know where I can get a train, do you?"

"I don't have much pull with the Union Pacific, I'm afraid. A country banker like me. But I can give you a letter of recommendation."

"That's all right, J.J. It would ruin me to be recommended by a banker. That's like being turned into a soprano. My national reputation would suffer. The reason my academy is drawing lawmen is my reputation, so I take great care to polish it and nurture it and add to it daily. It's my livelihood now."

"Well, for my money, you're the all-time greatest crook we've ever seen, and that includes Billy the Kid, Mugs."

"J.J., we're going to get along fine. I will let you know the date and time of the heist, and if you're nervous about your cash, you just lock it up. And of course, we'll be considerate of any customers in the place."

"Yes, that's a good idea, Mugs."

"I had *The Tattler* print up a card for me, and here it is. The lady at *The Tattler* and I have a warm and cheerful business arrangement."

"Very good, Mister Birdsong. We'll be in touch."

Mugs stepped into a fine day, with the dry breezes lifting his spirits. He meandered over to the orphanage, now the Academy of Crime, and noted the orphan siding that had once enabled the orphanage to unload freight and foundlings within a few yards of the building. It would be perfect. The orphanage was an inspired choice. He beamed at everyone in town, and they in turn lifted their straw boaters as they passed, or averted their gaze demurely.

Not far west of the orphanage was the Union Pacific yard, where old crews finished up and new crews boarded the trains. It didn't take Mugs long to figure out that everything was on hand for the first crime academy session. He needed an express car, and found two, plus a baggage car if he couldn't get an express car. And up ahead was an engine yard and coaling station, where engines were coaled, greased, watered, and serviced. There were several spare locomotives around, which suited him just fine.

He was looking over an express car when a railroad dick loomed before him.

"Whatcha doing?" the dick asked.

"Looking over an express car to rob," Mugs said. "You think this one here would work?"

"It ain't easy to knock over an express car," the dick said, chewing on the slimy remains of his cigar. The railroad dick was enjoying the encounter. He wore square-toed boots designed for ass-kicking, thick tan britches, a blue flannel shirt, black suspenders, and a battered black bowler. He had bright blue eyes, which now surveyed Mugs with increasing delight.

"Well, well, well," he said.

"Yeah, it's me, Wolfie," Mugs said. "Fancy meeting you here."

"I hear you got a crime school up and running," Wolfie said.

"Yeah, and you can help me. I need an express car to knock over. And a locomotive. And maybe a caboose."

"Those ain't easy to nip, Mugs baby."

"Here's what you do, Wolfie. You get me everything I need to do railroad heists, and run in to the orphan siding. Just park all that stuff there. I won't need the key to the express car...I'll show them how to blow it open. A little powder in the right places, that door caves right in."

"Ain't this a treat," Wolfie said. "Hey, Mugs, I want your autograph."

"My John Henry? I never got beyond printing in the sixth grade."

"You're gonna sign, Mugs baby. I want ten autographed Wanted posters. I can sell them. I get people from all over the place wiring me. They want to know if they could buy a Mugs Birdsong dodger, especially signed. Big Money, Mugs. I can sell them for twenty clams apiece."

"You want to go into business, Wolfie? I sign the wanted dodgers, and get two thirds, and you get a third."

"Naw, if you want an express car here, along with some steam, or a caboose, you gotta give me a mess of them dodgers, all signed by you. Do you know what you're worth? Millions and millions. I could sell ten thousand Wanted posters for twenty clams, if you sign them."

"Well, cut me in and I'll sign."

"Naw," said Wolfie. "I'll do the signing. I can sign your name better than I can sign my own. And you hardly know how to print letters."

For a moment, Mugs pondered the unruly universe. He'd been outmatched for once. It brought him a momentary sadness. But not for long.

"You're working for the Union Pacific, right? Here's the deal. I'm running monthly courses in crime. So, six times a year, when I give you the word, you run an express car, engine and caboose onto my siding, and I'll give you ten signed Mugs Birdsong Wanted posters. You'll get rich, Wolfie."

"It's a deal, Mugsy. But I want ten signed Wanted posters in advance."

"There's something more I want, Wolfie. You married?"

"Hell no. I own the town cathouse."

"Well, that'll work. I need a woman."

"We all do, Mugs."

"No, I mean for my classroom. I need to show how to snatch a woman for white slavery...you know, bind her up and get out and delivered. And I need a woman to teach purse snatching. And a woman when I teach pick-pocketing. Picking a woman's pocket ain't the same as picking a man's pocket. Stuff like that."

"Hell, I'll sell you one, Mugs."

"Naw, but if you could send one over when I need one, you'd make a few dollars on it."

Things were sure looking good, Mugs thought. He still needed to line up a few more items. Rustling was a big topic, and he'd need to show the lawmen how to alter brands, how to maverick, how to slide stolen stock out of a county and into stock cars. Eastern lawmen might not be as interested in rustling as the locals. Maybe he should offer a rustling course only every other session.

The Academy of Crime would open its doors in two days, and Mugs was almost ready. He could use an expert in tax dodging, moonshining, saloon fighting, and a few things like that, but he could teach any of those items. He had the experience but was better known as a bank robber. A little publicity would fix that.

IV

Wolfie's scheming bothered Mugs. The man might make a profit from Mugs's own Wanted posters. That would be sad. He wanted all of the poster business; there was no sense sharing his image with anyone.

But Typhoid Mary could help.

"Typhoid," he said after the obligatory cuddling, "I need some help."

"You sure do," she said. "It takes ten of you to equal one man."

"There's something you can do for me, and make some moolah, too. My problem is, my popularity is fading. I've been in the pen five years, and people have short memories, and there's a lot of people who hardly even heard of Mugs Birdsong. Unless I do something quick, my fifteen minutes of fame are up. And that's where you come in. Typhoid baby, we're going to restore my image worldwide."

"You're no good in bed," she said, "so that won't be easy."

"How you wound a man who's been in jail and had nothing by way of romance but a few knotholes, Typhoid. Here's the drill. You'll print all sorts of new Wanted Dead or Alive posters, and also some ten-thousand-dollar Reward posters. I'll autograph some, and you can sell those at a profit, by putting ads in *The Tattler*.

But most of them should be shipped out to sheriff departments across the country. Stir the pot a little."

"So, who's going to pay for all this?"

"I already have, baby. Coochie-coochie-coo."

"I should print my own Mugs Birdsong posters. Man Wanted."

"How you do sting me, Typhoid. Here's the scoop. It happens that I remember most of the lawmen who were chasing me from one county to another. Like Harold Nussbaum, down in Carson City. He wanted me for extortion, bank robbery, and littering, and he offered a reward. So we'll just revive it. Print me up some dodgers that say two-thousand-dollar reward for information leading to the arrest and conviction of Mugs Birdsong, and sign it Harold Nussbaum, sheriff. I'll sign a few for you to sell to fans, and you ship the rest across the country, so it gets pinned up in post offices and all that."

"What for?"

"I want to bask in fame the rest of my life, Typhoid."

"You're not famous with me, Mugs. I've done better."

"You're the best, Typhoid. You're a lulu. Now here's what I want. Wanted for Felony Arson, Sheriff Burt Baumgartner, Rapid City, South Dakota. Wanted for Kidnapping and Extortion, Sheriff Willard Bonack, Billings, Montana. Wanted Dead or Alive, Murder, Assault, Rustling, Cruelty to Animals, Failure to Register as a Mob Boss, Sheriff Wayne Wank, Albuquerque, New Mexico. Got that? We'll start with those and up the ante when these wear out. I've got a lot of worse ones if you dig a little."

"That's not very impressive," she said.

"Well, I plan to start small and build."

"That's how you always start," she said.

There was no dealing with the woman. Mugs got out of the sack, dressed, and left, while Typhoid grinned.

It was time to come up with a curriculum. After all, the lawmen would be arriving the next day, and he needed a plan of instruction. He also wanted them to have a good time, so between

crime talk there would be lemonade and cookies, and introduc-
tions to society ladies, and directions to the opium parlor on the
south side of the tracks.

He decided that the first sessions would be devoted to theft of
various sorts, and the later sessions would be devoted to assault and
murder and kidnapping, though he wasn't sure whether kidnapping
was a theft or an assault. It didn't matter. By the time he was done,
these lawmen would have an intimate knowledge of all manner of
crime, taught by an expert.

He'd start with something spectacular. The bank robbery would
do just fine. He'd let J.J. Jones know that the heist would happen at
nine the next morning.

He drifted down to the Union Pacific station, a wooden
structure on the main line, and waited for his pigeons to arrive.
Most of them would arrive on the afternoon West Coast Limited,
and the rest would drift in on other trains. It sure was a fine day,
with lots of sunshine and a good breeze. He could teach outside.
There was nothing worse than classrooms full of sweaty armpits.

The train huffed in only ten minutes late, a miracle by U.P.
standards, and, sure enough, first off the Pullman was Oscar "Bull"
Arbuckle, the toughest lawman in west Texas. Bull was famous
for shooting the notorious gambler Rafe Routinger after Rafe had
knocked him flat on the floor and threatened to kick the sheriff to
death. But Bull had rolled sideways, kicked his legs up, and shot the
gambler using his holstered revolver. The episode had been trum-
peted by the *Police Gazette*.

"Welcome, Bull," Mugs said.

"Well, well, well," Bull said.

Next off the car was Cannonball Moses, bull-necked sheriff
of Prescott, Arizona, and friend of the Earp boys. Cannonball was
famous for his physical prowess. He scarcely ever used a firearm,
preferring to wade in and plant massive fists into the middle of
whoever he was dealing with.

"Welcome to Rock Springs, Cannonball."

"Well, well, well," Cannonball said.

His handshake was so massive that Mugs worried that his fingers were broken.

Next off the sleeper car was Whispering Winger, sheriff of Jim Jones County, Texas. Whispering was the sneakiest lawman in the profession, with the ability to make himself almost invisible. He could stand on a sidewalk as a pure nonentity, hearing crime on the winds, and corralling the culprits before they were got to pay dirt.

"Mugs Birdsong, well, well, well," he whispered.

Mugs was getting bored and thought he would be better off in some other profession, but he had chosen an academic life, so he felt he had to proceed, and give these lawmen their money's worth. Or rather, their taxpayers' money's worth, since none of them were schooling themselves on their own dime.

One by one, they stepped down to the gravel platform. There was Walker Wall, the last Civil War veteran still operating as a peace officer, and Seamus Bullwinkle, one of only two Easterners this time around. He was a police captain in the Hell's Kitchen precinct of New York. And, of course, Andy Apple, the banjoist in a lawmen's quartet called Sing Sing. Mugs liked Andy, even though Andy had sent Mugs up the river for seven months back in 'Eighty-Nine.

They drifted in on the next three passenger trains, including one from California that brought mustachioed Hernando Growler, the scourge of Chinatown. Growler had been Mugs's nemesis three times, and accounted for thirteen months of Mugs's lifetime accumulation of seventeen years' jail time.

Mugs steered each arrival to his room in the orphanage, and invited the lawmen down to the dining room for the opening reception, which was presided over by Sally Sortelege, madam of the local palace of delights.

As the evening wore on, and the lawmen got mellow, Mugs spread out some fresh Wanted dodgers and signed them. They had congregated in the orphanage dining area, but some of the bottles lining one table would never have been opened for orphans. It was time to welcome the lawmen.

"Gents," he said, "welcome to Rock Springs, Wyoming, home of the Mugs Birdsong Academy of Crime. We're going to lead off tomorrow with a special event, a heist at our local bank. Its president, J.J. Jones, has eagerly co-operated in the enterprise, and the cash drawers will be stuffed with fake two dollar bills, courtesy of *The Tattler* printing outfit. Now, we need to divide into two teams. The robbers and the lawmen. I will instruct the robbers in the fine art of knocking over a bank, and the lawmen will congregate in the offices of our sheriff, Mister Stoopnagle, who is here this eve, and it will be up to the lawmen to stop the crime, and recover the boodle. Remember to use blanks. Anyone who uses real ammo will be flunked and sent home. Remember...blanks only."

They all looked mighty cheerful.

"Now, I have prepared some souvenirs for you to take home after completing the course work. On the table, there are several Mugs Birdsong Wanted dodgers, which I have autographed. The proceeds go to my favorite charity. They are only two bucks each, and you're gonna take several, and give them to your children and relatives for Christmas. Sally, here, will take your pocket change and give you a receipt and a brass token good for a half-price quickie at her palace of delights."

It all went smoothly. Mugs sent word to J.J. Jones that his bank would be knocked over at nine, following the pancake breakfast, and Jones replied that he'd be delighted. Mugs collected the ten bank robbers and issued instructions. One was to keep watch on the sheriff office, and if the lawmen in there erupted, he was to signal the rest of the robbers with three rapid shots. Mugs had fast get-away nags ready, and some canvas sacks for the loot, and a string of Chinese firecrackers for diversionary purposes. The look-out was to set these off a block away.

"Now, a lot depends on the tellers. You've got to scare them into emptying the cash drawers fast. If they put up any resistance, you've got to get into the cage and hog-tie them. If the lawmen show up, it's necessary to take them hostage. You'll need spare horses for that. Don't cut them loose until you're free and clear of town, and not until you've pulled ahead of the posse."

"Who's playing the tellers?" Hernando asked.

"They are themselves. Be sure not to wound them, or J.J. Jones will be unhappy."

"What's this supposed to teach us?" Hernando asked. "What's in this that we don't already know about heists?"

"Experience," Mugs said. "You're going through the whole drill, and planning the heist from the get-go."

"I think I'm gonna want a refund," he said.

"If you're not entirely satisfied by the end of the term, you can apply for a refund," Mugs said. "No one leaves the academy unrewarded. Over in the sheriff's office the lawmen are studying how to respond to the heist and collect a posse and go after you."

"Big deal," said Hernando.

They worked out the heist well into the evening, and then had a nightcap with the lawmen, and went to their orphanage rooms, which were pretty small cubicles.

Mugs went to Typhoid's cottage feeling dissatisfied. This whole bank robbery deal wasn't working out as well as he had hoped. He figured he would have to come up with something that would surprise both the robbers and lawmen, but he couldn't imagine what.

The next morning, after a fine pancake breakfast, the students split into the two groups, and the robbers prepared to knock over the bank, while the lawmen prepared to stop them.

Mugs went along to coach the robbers, but they really didn't need any coaching. They posted a man near the sheriff office; they lined up the get-away horses around the corner from the bank, and they pulled on bandanna masks and barged in at the stroke of nine.

No sooner did they enter the lobby than a pail of water splashed over them, half a dozen lariats looped out, lassoing them, J.J. Jones began firing blanks from an old Navy revolver, the two tellers jabbed the robbers with billy clubs and refused to fill up the sacks, and then the law contingent arrived with the look-out and the horse holder neatly hog-tied, and all the get-away horses under their control.

Worse, the town's merchants arrived and started a fist fight in the bank lobby, and Hernando lost a tooth. Cannonball bloodied a lip. Whispering cracked a skull. After that, the sheriff, Stoopnagle, arrived with two deputies and pinched all the students for disorderly conduct, and hauled the whole lot to the jail, smiling to beat the band. All twenty students paid the two-dollar fine and then hit the saloons.

The Rock Springs Academy of Crime was off to a rocky start. But maybe things would get better.

V

Mugs Birdsong soon discovered he didn't have much to say. In fact, once he stood in front of some savvy lawmen he discovered that they knew more than he did. When he tried to demonstrate purse snatching, the peace officers soon were bored. They knew all that stuff.

"Tell us something we don't know, Mugs!" one yelled.

"I'm working on it," he said uneasily. The course wasn't going as planned.

When he began to discuss burglary, and break-ins, the lawmen knew more ways to bust into any building than he did. In a way, that rescued the day. He had little to teach them, but they had plenty to teach each other, and all he had to do was get them to talking, and exchanging experiences. Mugs was a quick study, and he was soon inviting members of his class to step up and talk about the cases they had busted — how to spot cat burglars at work, or how to thwart jewel thieves, or where to lurk when nailing a mugger in a park.

Pretty soon, all those sterling coppers were teaching each other. All Mugs did was start the ball rolling, and then the lawmen plunged in, each with a story that outdid anyone else's. Hernando told about how he caught three whores drowning a drunk in a hot springs spa, and Whispering told about how he saw a robbery of a post office about to happen, and thwarted it by swinging a mail sack at a crook. Cannonball recounted the time he saw some vagrants in an alley behind a pawn shop, saw that two of them were about to slit the throat of a banker, and chased the two into a carnival, where they tried to hide in a brown bear's cage and got mauled.

Good stuff, and every man had contributions to make. Mugs never saw such a happy bunch, exchanging war stories hour after hour. Maybe his Academy of Crime would be a success after all. They did that for two weeks. Men who were strangers when they first gathered became old friends. They bought each other drinks when the class shut down each afternoon.

But Mugs knew it wasn't going to last much longer, certainly not the month he had allocated for the course work.

So he simply shortened the term.

"Gents, we've covered everything I planned to teach over the term, and now it's time to give you your diplomas. Tomorrow we'll do one last drill...a train robbery. I've arranged for an engine, an express car, and a caboose to be run onto the siding just outside, and we'll figure out how to rob the express car."

"Hot diggity," said Whispering.

"I've always wanted to blow a train wide open," said Hernando. "Man, this makes the academy worthwhile."

"The express car's almost impenetrable," Mugs said. "And so is the safe inside. These days, train robbers can't simply bust in and ride off with a bundle of greenbacks. But your task is to find out how to do it."

"We'll need some powder," said Cannonball.

"I've got all that," Mugs said.

Sure enough, Wolfie was as good as his word. Early the next morning, the engine and cars backed into the siding and parked in front of the orphanage. A bored engineer and fireman sat in the diamond-stacked old freight engine, and a couple of Union Pacific brakemen snoozed cheerfully in the caboose.

The heist was set for nine in the morning; at ten, the class was to gather and discuss what went right and wrong, and draw some conclusions.

Mugs just smiled and nodded. "This is your final exam, gents. Do it right and you all get an A."

"And what'll flunk us?" someone wanted to know.

"That train's due to pull out at nine-fifteen. If it goes, with the express car door closed, and the safe untouched, you all flunk."

"Whooee," said Hernando.

At nine, several lawmen crawled up to the express car, laid powder against the door, fused the powder and lit it, while two others climbed into the cab intending to open the valves and empty the steam, but the U.P. men met them with coal shovels and beat them back. Two more lawmen jumped the caboose, and were invited to coffee by the brakemen. Then the powder blew, but it didn't budge the express car door. Instead it knocked out seventeen windows in the orphanage. The engineer threw the engine into action, and it began pulling out of the siding while the fireman threw shovel-loads of hot ashes at the bandits, burning the faces of three lawmen.

After that, the sorry lawmen collected in the newly ventilated orphanage for a recap of the crime.

"You gonna flunk us, Mugs?" asked one.

"Give yourself a grade," Mugs said.

"It ain't easy, a life of crime," said Hernando.

"I've got to admire you, Mugs," said Whispering. "Crime's a lot harder than I thought. I always supposed it was lazy buggers did these jobs, but it's hard work, and trouble all the way. If I learned anything from the academy, it's that crooks work a lot harder than I do. Than all of us do. Man, oh, man, I'm not fit to be a crook."

"Me, I learned how tough it is to be a crook," Hernando said. "I got burnt, clubbed, beaten, and defeated. Criminals, they're some kind of geniuses, or they don't survive. No wonder so many go straight. They don't cut the mustard."

"Well, then, you've learned something," Mugs said. "I've been preparing for a life of crime from the day I was born. Even before I could read and write, I was learning the art, mastering the techniques. By the time I was seven, I'd stolen a grand piano, and by the age of twelve I had sold four women into white slavery. By the time I was twenty I'd robbed twelve banks and blown open six railway express cars. It took courage, skill, dedication, and a lot of faith to become the greatest crook of all time.

"And that's what you've learned here. Being a crook is a calling, something profound and idealistic. Now you've seen for yourselves what goes into becoming a legend."

"Yeah, man, you're the master, all right," said Bull Arbuckle, with admiration.

"You are all going to be masters of crime," Mugs said. "The course ain't long enough to turn you into doctors. So here's your diplomas."

He handed each lawman a diploma. "Fill in your name. I don't spell so good."

It was wondrous to behold. All those lawmen sat down and began penning their names into the diplomas, looking mighty satisfied.

Cannonball Moses spoke for all of them. "Mugs, this has been the most valuable and important two weeks of my life. Thanks to you, I've gone from being a local sheriff to someone who's studied with a world-renowned master criminal, up there with Jack the Ripper. I want you to know, we'll be talking this up, insisting that every lawman in the country attend your academy, and learn at your feet. I speak for all of us in wishing you every success. You've transformed our lives."

"Amen," said those dedicated lawmen.

Mugs sure enjoyed the heartfelt endorsement. He got off on the wrong foot, didn't know what to teach, finally let them teach themselves, and now they all were telling him he was the finest crook in all creation.

He helped them pack, and escorted them to the railroad station, and shook hands as they caught passenger trains east and west. He saw them settle in their seats in the coaches, and pull out their diplomas to admire them. He thought he saw some moist eyes, but couldn't be sure because the train windows were grimy. When all had left, Mugs had a tender moment of loss, already missing all those fine lawmen who had brightened his life.

Mugs felt mighty happy. He'd turned a long course into a two-week one and no one demanded a refund. And word of mouth would fill the ranks of students for years to come. Indeed, some of them had left written endorsements for Mugs to use any time he saw fit. He thought he'd take them over to Typhoid Mary and have her turn them into a sales brochure.

The bills rolled in fast. It cost $37 to replace the windows in the orphanage. The Union Pacific sent him a bill for $53, which paid for repairing and repainting the damaged express car door. A mess of other bills floated in. The food service in the orphanage kitchen came to $60; laundering sheets and cleaning twenty rooms in the orphanage came to $50. Some minor repairs to woodwork at the bank came to $31. The railroad sent a second bill, this one for coal used up in putting the train on the siding, but that was only $11. Typhoid Mary stuck him with half a dozen invoices for Wanted posters, brochures, and advertising, and that came to $121. That wounded him. He thought he was repaying her handsomely, lover boy that he was.

He laid this mess of bills and invoices on his table, and sighed. Then he headed for the bank, where J.J. Jones quickly informed him he had enough to cover all those expenses, with a few dollars to spare — if no more bills floated in. He had done all that work for just a few dollars. He'd gotten lots of compliments, but you can't live on compliments, and now he was nearly broke again.

He contemplated doing a quick stick-up and returning to the pen, where he would be warmly welcomed. It was a temptation. Life was hard. Going straight was harder. A life of crime was the better choice for him, and now he seriously considered it. He thought he'd see what Typhoid Mary might think about it. He bared his heart to her when they lay side-by-side each night, though she kept her thoughts entirely to herself. Maybe he should kill her and take over the newspaper. Then he could print his own brochures and not get billed.

The more he contemplated what to do, the more tempted he was to rob the bank. How could he go wrong? He had the run of the place. He could walk in and shake the paw of J.J. Jones himself. He knew the tellers by their first name. They'd all come to trust him and believe he was going straight, and was another fine howdy-do citizen.

He decided to wait a bit; he didn't need moolah. He was mooching off Typhoid Mary; his bills were paid; he didn't have to hire lawyers to spring him from confinement. So he began planning his next session, noticing with delight that seven of the student lawmen had caught him and sent him up the river.

There was Filibuster Smith of Santa Fe, who had caught him in a con when he was trying to blackmail a wealthy Mexican widow out of ten grand. That had cost him fifteen months. There was Cyrus Maguire, the dreaded sheriff of Leadville, Colorado, who had caught him fleeing from a bank with over $200,000 in hundreds and fifties. That had cost him three to five, and he served almost five. There was Amos Turk, chief of police of Las Vegas, New Mexico, who nabbed him in the middle of a stick-up of a rich lawyer. That cost eleven months.

There was also Muttonchop Ames, the deputy sheriff at Silver City, New Mexico, who caught him trying to liberate half a million dollars of silver bullion in a commandeered train. That cost four months, because the judge had been paid off. There were three others: Bailey Bain, Dodge City's beat policeman, who had collared him, Joe Studebaker, undersheriff of Tucson, and Marley Drake, the worst of all, who caught him with a smoking gun in hand after he had killed his business partner, Deadeye Dick Dole.

It sure was a bonanza. All these men arriving together, his nemeses, the very ones who had defeated him in his lifelong quest to succeed. Maybe, with luck, he could do something about all that.

VI

Mugs was restless. The next class wasn't due for a while. His Wanted Dead or Alive posters were floating around the country, improving his notoriety. He had become a local hero in Rock Springs, where his academy was improving the economy.

But it was all a yawn. Whenever he got bored, he looked for something to steal. The trouble was, he had stolen almost everything, so it was no longer a mental challenge. If you've done it all, what is there to aspire to?

He considered knocking off a bank or two, or going after an express car on the Union Pacific, or swindling someone out of a gold mine. One idea appealed to him, which was stealing from mobsters. He'd let them do the dealing, and then take it all away. But that bored him, too; he'd done that, along with everything else he could conjure up.

He was really growing desperate in Rock Springs; maybe he should close the academy and head for southern California, and steal from actors. Maybe he should just arrange to get caught at something, and get sent up for a while, so he wouldn't have to worry about his retirement. He had no pension, but the state penitentiary would handle all that.

Then he realized there was something after all that he had

never stolen. He had never stolen another man's wife. The more he pondered that, the more entertaining was the prospect. One could not be the complete criminal without some wife-stealing.

He decided to try some serious wife-swiping, but he needed to define the terms. What was wife-stealing? And was there a big prize, or were all wife thefts the same? Was wife-stealing simply bedding someone's wife, or was it winning the lady's affections? Did divorce matter? Was stealing a beautiful, desirable, celebrated wife worth more in the scale of things than stealing someone's little woman?

He toyed with all this, and gradually came to some conclusions. Since he was the most notorious criminal in the country, he had to do a spectacular theft. No rinky-dink theft would do. He would need to steal someone socially prominent, someone celebrated for her talent and beauty, someone attached to someone powerful and important, and the theft would need to be complete. He'd have to walk away with the lady.

The whole idea enchanted him. If he was already a notorious thief, imagine what stealing such a woman would do for him. Stealing three or four would help, but if he stole fifty, he would garner some real fame and not be just an also-ran. He would go down in history. He would be known, not only in the republic, but abroad. They would whisper about him in London. He would outstrip the most daring cads in Paris. He would make the Italians look impotent, and the Spanish look neutered. He would make that Bolivian, Porfirio Fuentes, look like an amateur.

The whole idea fermented and boiled and steamed in his head, absorbing him so much he forgot he was in Rock Springs, Wyoming, awaiting the arrival of the next class in a couple of weeks.

Rock Springs hardly seemed the place to start, and he thought to hop a freight train for Salt Lake, where he might find all manner of women, but he finally settled on Rock Springs for experimental purposes. It would be a training ground, that would prepare him for some serious wife-stealing in New York, or New Orleans.

But where to start? He began casing the town. It was largely male. Such women that he found on the streets were married to railroad workers or miners, and half of them were expecting a third or fourth child. Plainly, that could get sticky. Having made the conquest, he would need to get rid of her and go on to the next. That meant finding someone a little older, perhaps. There were things here he knew nothing about, having enjoyed the hospitality of penitentiaries most of his adult life.

He thought about the wives of successful merchants, and eyed their houses and glimpsed them in their neighborhoods, but that led nowhere. He tried the saloons, but found no likely prospect there. He could manage a liaison with all sorts of women, but stealing one from a prominent husband was something else, and he was on new turf. The world's greatest crook was a rank amateur in the realm of wife-nipping.

But then good fortune struck. He was palling around with his friend J.J. Jones at the bank one day when Jones's wife walked in. She was a fine, slim forty, with wide-set innocent eyes, well-manicured hands, silky brown hair that had recently been combed, and a swift smile.

"Ah, my dear, meet my friend Mugs Birdsong," J.J. Jones said, when she stepped into his office. "Mugs, meet my wife, Jill Jane Jones, also known as J.J."

"Two double Js in one family. It's unheard of," Mugs said.

"That's why we married," the banker said. "If you want J.J. Jones, you get two for one."

The wifely one accepted Mugs's slightly unclean paw, shook it, and smiled dubiously.

"Madam, you are a wonder, and the shining light of Rock Springs," Mugs said, being as gallant as he could manage.

"Coming from a famous badman, I treasure your sentiment," she said.

"Yes, the word of an international crook carries more weight than a run-of-the-mill one," Mugs said.

"I didn't know you were an international crook," she said.

"There are Wanted Dead or Alive posters all about me in Canada and Mexico, and at least two in England, and one in Japan," he said. "Plus, the French are about to add me to their list of arch-criminals."

"You must feel proud. We're so lucky to have you in little old Rock Springs," she said.

"It was the empty orphanage, ma'am. I saw my chance in it."

"Well, do stop in for tea some afternoon," she said.

"Keep an eye on your silver," he replied. "And count the spoons after I leave."

She laughed merrily, and so did the banker.

"You're a true rascal," Jones said.

"You don't know the half of it," Mugs replied. "There's nothing I won't swipe."

Jones laughed heartily.

"Well, dear, I'll leave you two men to your bookkeeping," Mrs. Jones said, and turned to leave. But she paused before Mugs and patted his unshaven cheek. "It's like having a tiger on the loose," she said. "Name your price, Mugs, and the town'll pay it."

Then she was gone. Mugs was dazed. There she was, the premium property in Rock Springs, and he had an invitation to stop by for tea. He could begin his pilferage at once, and complete it before the next class arrived at the academy.

He worried about tea. He could not remember what tea tasted like. Tea was for people as unlike himself as people get. Would it make him fart? He resolved to sip it gingerly at first, until he got the hang of tea drinking and was certain it was safe.

Mugs headed for Typhoid Mary's, poured some water from the pitcher into the porcelain wash basin, and began scrubbing his hands. He found a bar of soap, lathered his hands, and rinsed them in the basin. The water was gray. He pitched that out the window, poured some more, and did it again, and this time the water was not so stained. But his fingernails were still black, and he didn't know how to clean them. He found a nail file among Typhoid's possessions, and used it as a pickaxe to pry the grime out from under his fingernails. He persisted until the nails were as clean as his hands, and then he washed all over again and threw the water out.

He debated whether to wash the rest of him, but decided against it. He didn't want to be too much of a dandy. Let her discover a he-man under his britches if it came to that. He couldn't remember an entire bath, toes to nose, since leaving the pen, and he didn't want to start anything new. He did, however, find a brush and took after his clothing, scraping away caked food and things beyond identification, and he scrubbed at an oily spot on his brown shirt, with little effect. And then he brushed his fedora, sweeping away a lot of grit and grime, and then he presented himself to a mirror at Typhoid's, found himself satisfactory for wooing purposes, and headed into a bright day. He knew exactly where the Jones house was; he had cased it several times, thinking to knock it over someday. It wasn't pretentious; nothing in Rock Springs, Wyoming, displayed any extravagance. But it was a solid, comfortable house befitting a rural banker, with a fine verandah, and windows that looked out upon the sere hills and bleak cliffs of the area.

She was a little surprised to see him, but she smiled.

"That was fast," she said. "Tea for two, right?"

"Does tea make you fart?" he asked.

She paused, smiled, and offered a reply. "Like an old mare," she said.

While she heated the tea on her coal stove, Mugs cased the place, seeing what could be lifted easily. There was some fancy art, but he didn't know good art from bad, so he ignored it. Still, he wouldn't mind copping the oil portrait of Jane Jill, or was it Jill Jane. It didn't matter when all he needed was to call her J.J. Same with some Wedgwood stuff. It was worth something, but he didn't know how to fence it in Rock Springs. Some oriental rugs were scattered around, but those would be tough to haul away and sell.

Pretty soon she brought a tray, the tea in a floral pot he thought might be Chinese and worth pinching. She poured, offered him sugar, which he turned down, wanting to taste tea unadulterated.

He burned his lips a little, and then got some in and swilled it around to clean his teeth, and then downed it. He evaluated it a moment, and saw her gazing, curiosity on her face.

"Well?" she asked.

"Cat piss," he said.

"You're an original, Mugs."

"You want to get laid?" he asked.

She set down her tea cup and stared, and then smiled.

"I knew there was something about you I'd like," she said.

"Yeah, well I don't beat around the bush," he said, trying another sip. He decided it needed some sugar, so poured a few spoonfuls in, stirred, and sipped again. "That's better," he said. "I don't like licorice, and I was gonna add tea to the list, but with some sugar things get better."

They sat in utter silence, each going through tea-sipping rituals, watching motes dance in the sunlight.

"Yeah, well, it's my reputation I'm worried about," he said. "You know who's got the biggest rep of all? Billy the Kid? Nah, it's me. Mugs Birdsong. Can you think of anyone comes close? Nah, not anyone alive or dead. I've done it all. You looking for a stagecoach bandit? Look no further. Train robber? I've stopped express trains and made off with gold bullion. You want a killer? You'd faint if I told you how many I'd killed. You want a pickpocket? Purse snatcher? Man, you should see me at work. I'm so smooth they don't know they've been hit for hours."

He was warming up to his favorite topic, himself, and she was rapt. All this tea stuff, it'd be just fine.

"Hey, assault. I've left a dozen women weeping. I've put fifty men in hospitals. I've cut the balls off a dozen. I've brained babies. I've robbed my best friends. I've butchered and eaten little girls."

She was smiling. Smiling and sipping.

"But you know, baby, there's one thing didn't get done, and I can't make the grade to all-time world-famous master criminal until I do it."

She stared.

"I've never stolen another man's wife, and I've decided you're it."

She smiled slightly.

"Yeah, babe, you're the first. I'm gonna steal you and then a few dozen more, the richer and prettier the better. I'm gonna steal wives from now until I croak."

"Not today, but I'll think about it," she said. "Mugs, you're a card."

VII

Mugs liked the bank robbery part of his crime school and decided to keep it. Everyone had fun. It was a fine way for lawmen to get to know one another. They laughed, and talked about it for the rest of the session. So he told the banker, J.J. Jones, that he was going to do it again on the first or second day of the next session.

"Be sure and lock up the real stuff in your vault, J.J., I don't want any accidents."

"That sure was fun, Mugs. I'm not worried, because it's lawmen doing it. But we'll take precautions. Let me know the hour."

"They'll be toasting you," Mugs said.

"I'll load the old Navy," said J.J. "Those wads sting when they hit someone, and that's half the fun of it."

Mugs promised to keep J.J. Jones posted, along with the tellers, and townspeople. It looked like the bank robbery was going to become a ritual opening celebration for each class. The hardware people were delighted to sell a lot of blank cartridges, so there'd be lots of noise. The whole town of Rock Springs could hardly wait for the next heist.

Mugs decided there wasn't enough fake money to satisfy the lawmen, so he corralled Typhoid, who ran a printing operation as well as *The Tattler*.

"I want a mess of fake money...fins, sawbucks, century notes, you name it. And on some good tough paper so it lasts," Mugs said.

"Anything for old lover boy," she said, leering at him. "Just return the favor...if you're capable."

She sure was mean, he thought.

She set to work, and soon had a pile of greenbacks, in all denominations, all neatly cut with her paper cutter, and stacked and counted. This stuff was much better than the first stuff, but it was still plainly toy money, and even said Fake where the president was supposed to be in the middle of each bill. But now there'd be a mess of greenbacks in the tills when the lawmen pulled off the heist.

Mugs took a pile of it over to J.J. The banker admired the greenbacks, and smiled.

"This'll make it more fun," he said. "I'll fill the cash trays with it at each cage, and we'll be ready."

"Just be sure you lock up the real stuff," Mugs said. "Every last dime."

"That's a promise, Mugs."

The banker had told Mugs that he usually kept eighty to a hundred thousand in cash on hand. The railroad used a lot of it to pay its workers, and local ranchers paid their drovers in cash, too. They all got greenbacks in brown envelopes on pay day.

"I'm gonna quit doing the express train robbery," he told J.J. "The railroad wanted too much to repair everything. So I'll just keep the rest of the session in the classrooms, and let the lawmen tell stories."

"Your crime school sure is a big boost for Rock Springs," the banker said.

"I got a lot of special guests this time," Mugs said. "Seven of the twenty sent me up the river. Between them, they cost me fifteen years. I want to show them a lot of consideration."

"You're an amazing man, Mugs. Taking kindly to the lawmen who put you in the slammer."

"Well, they'll learn from my school," Mugs said. "I hope they'll be better at their task when we're done."

"No doubt about it," the banker said.

The time of the next session finally arrived, and Mugs dutifully headed for the Union Pacific station to welcome the arriving lawmen. The westbound train huffed in, and Mugs soon found himself shaking the paw of Muttonchop Ames, and then Filibuster Smith.

"Well, well, well," said Smith.

"Reception this eve. Just settle yourselves in any of the rooms at that schoolhouse over yonder," Mugs said.

"You gonna teach me something I don't know?" Ames said.

"Naw, mostly I sit back and let you gents teach each other."

Ames smiled. "Where's the nearest watering hole?"

Mugs pointed. In fact, he pointed this way and that, and in six or eight directions, because that was Rock Springs for you.

The next train brought Cyrus Maguire and Amos Turk, and he shook hands with these two, who remembered Mugs.

"Well, well, well," said Turk. "You haven't changed at all."

"Same as ever," Mugs said.

They all laughed.

Next train deposited Bailey Bain, Joe Studebaker, and Marley Drake on the station platform, and several other lawmen Mugs hadn't met. But he welcomed them all, steered them to the orphanage, told them to take a room, and be ready for the reception that evening.

"Liquid refreshments?" Drake asked.

"Anything that can be smoked or drunk," Mugs said.

They all wandered off cheerfully, and most spent the remainder of that opening day inspecting Rock Springs saloons with an expert eye. Any lawman worth his salt could examine a saloon, know what sort of clientele it had, and who to arrest.

The opening reception was scheduled for the cocktail hour, so Mugs made sure the orphanage was well supplied with bottles.

"Gents," he said, when all had wandered into the orphanage

dining area, "this here is our local sheriff, Barney Stoopnagle. He's our host this evening. We always start our course of instruction with a bank robbery, and he'll tell you exactly what will happen. We're going to divide our forces into two teams...the robbers and the lawmen. The only rule is to use blanks in your revolvers. No one gets hurt. Out of all this you will take away with you a fine, subtle, brilliant grasp of bank robbery, that will equip you to stop real bank robberies in their tracks, simply because you'll know exactly what the criminals will do next.

"Now I'm going to appoint the two teams. The bank robbers will include Filibuster Smith, Cyrus Maguire, Amos Turk, Muttonchop Ames, Bailey Bain, Joe Studebaker, and Marley Drake. The rest of you will be on the lawman team, attempting to stop the bank robbery and thwart the get-away. And with that, gents, I give you Sheriff Stoopnagle."

Barney stood up, did a few "aw shucks", and began welcoming the lawmen to Rock Springs. "We're glad you're here," he said. "You improve our crime rate. When twenty lawmen are bunking in the old orphanage, we don't even see a cat being tortured by a brat."

Mugs sighed happily, vanished from the room, made his way swiftly to the darkened bank, let himself in with a key he had snagged, opened the vault with the combination he had memorized, removed the packets of real greenbacks fresh from the Treasury, and placed these in a Gladstone bag. He replaced these with phony packets, each with a real greenback top and bottom, but otherwise stacked with Typhoid Mary's toy money. These he returned to the vault. The cash trays for the tellers' wickets had been readied for the next morning's heist, and he mixed a few real greenbacks in with the fake stuff, closed the vault, left the bank, headed for the express office where he shipped the Gladstone to a certain address in the Principality of Monaco, using a tag he'd nipped weeks earlier, and watched briefly as the eastbound huffed its way out of Rock Springs. He was back at the reception thirty-four minutes later, having missed his goal by four minutes, for which he scolded himself.

He was about eighty thousand dollars richer.

He soon was mixing and mingling with all those fine lawmen, who spent a bibulous evening getting to know one another. In time, the evening grew ripe, and it was time to shut things down.

"Gents, he said, "tomorrow we'll do the exercise. Pay attention. Learn what you can about bank heists and how to prevent them. Everything's ready. The get-away horses will be in place, ready for the horse holder. Choose your look-out, decide how you'll knock over the bank. Take notes. I'll be with my friend Sheriff Stoopnagle in his offices, awaiting your results. He or I can act as a referee if needed. But this is all your baby...and don't forget to enjoy your-selves. It's not everyone who gets to play a bank robber."

With that, all those fine officers of the law headed for their bunks, save for a few who wished to go a round or two more in the local saloons.

Mugs slept soundly.

The next morning, the whole town was ready to get in on the fun. The heist began at nine, and before long some brats were tossing strings of Chinese firecrackers under the get-away horses, causing equine panic, so most of the horses bolted, leaving the horse handler at a loss to fetch them back for the get-away.

The robbers barged into the bank, revolvers drawn, bandannas covering their nostrils, and soon swept piles of greenery into their canvas sacks, all of it gotten from the two cash drawers in the teller cages. But the tellers fought back, using billy clubs to whack at fingers and wrists. J.J. Jones pulled out his old Navy Colt and began blasting away, the wads whacking into the foreheads and chins of the robbers. A shoeshine boy walked in during the robbery, and offered to shine the boots of the robbers, and when they said they were busy, he started jeering at them.

Jones calmly reloaded, pouring powder down the cylinders, following with fresh wads, and putting caps over nipples, and then began blasting away at Cyrus Maguire, who had taken his fancy, and managed to put a wad into Maguire's eyebrow, which reddened and swelled.

Town merchants set up a trip line on the bank stairs, so when the bank robbers poured out, they tripped, and went bounding downs the stairs, topsy-turvy, spilling some toy money, which the good citizens of Rock Springs promptly commandeered. Joe Studebaker landed on his nose and it dripped red. Marley Drake began banging away at citizens, and was making fierce noises when two merchants jumped him from behind, knocking him flat. They stole a handful of toy money and scattered it like confetti. Little girls snatched it up.

After that, the thirteen other academy students, acting as lawmen, captured the bank robbers, hog-tied them, and hauled them off to the orphanage while half the citizens of Rock Springs hooted. It sure was a rout.

The get-away horses, still spooked, were finally corralled and returned to the livery barn, and Rock Springs settled down to a quiet summer day. Mugs and Sheriff Stoopnagle meandered over to the classrooms to begin course instruction. The first day would include train robbery, mugging, purse snatching, pickpocketing, and drinks at five.

Mugs addressed the students.

"Well, we've had our fun, and now it's time to get busy with some serious stuff. Let's start with train robbery. Have any of you dealt with a train robbery?"

"Yep," said Amos Turk. "They robbed a baggage car, walked through the passenger cars lifting cash and jewelry, and rode off."

"How'd you deal with it?" Mugs asked.

"Formed a posse and shot the bastards."

"How did you know where to go?"

"They'd quit their horses, flagged an eastbound freight, hopped the caboose, and we figured it out. Crooks are lazy."

"Doesn't sound very bright," Mugs said.

J.J. Jones burst into the classroom, looking wild-eyed and crazy. "We've been robbed. The bank's been robbed!" he cried, waving a packet of bills.

The lawmen laughed. Plainly, this was the last act of the morning's fun.

"Sirs!" Jones cried. "I am not funning you. My bank's been robbed. My tellers discovered it. The vault's been ransacked. Fake packets. The real money's gone. Eighty thousand dollars, our entire cash reserves, give or take a few bills."

It was hard for all these lawmen, who'd been cavorting at the bank only a short while before, to come to grips with it. But Jones was not fooling.

"Where have you looked?" Mugs asked.

"Everywhere!"

"Might the cash have been left in the tellers' trays?"

"No, sir. Those were emptied."

"Was the money left in the vault, or put elsewhere for safe-keeping?" Mugs asked.

Sheriff Stoopnagle rose. "All right, I'll look into it," he said. "You gents stay out of it. I don't want twenty hothouse flowers messing me up. Someone around Rock Springs is a crook and I will find him. Mister Jones, I'll have the cash back to you shortly."

VIII

They watched the huffy old sheriff leave, with J.J. Jones in tow. There might be twenty top lawmen sitting there, but the sheriff wanted no part of them. He was going to solve it his own way.

Mugs was enchanted.

"We've got a real case. And you're going to solve it," he said. "Maybe we can do it right here, in this classroom."

"Fat chance," said Filibuster Smith.

"If twenty top lawdogs can't solve it, you should turn in your badges," Mugs said.

That got them. A swift change of mood in the room told Mugs that all twenty were raring to go.

"All right. We need to reconstruct the crime and build a list of suspects," Mugs said.

"You're the expert," Filibuster Smith said.

"Now, just to put things on the table, let's do the suspects. I am your prime suspect. I'm the most notorious criminal in the country. I could use the loot. But you're all suspects, too. You were present during the heist. Some of you emptied the tellers' cash trays. Others of you were milling around. Some might be accessories, some worse. So, we now have twenty-one names, and you'll be investigating yourselves and me."

"Cut the crap, Birdsong," said Joe Studebaker. "We'll be looking at you, not us. We're the law."

"You have a point. Actually, the prime suspects are the two tellers. Someone got into the vault, took real cash, and put the fake packets in there, the ones with toy money inside, and real bills outside. That makes it an inside job. But they still needed someone to take away the real stuff during the heist."

"Sure, and maybe J.J. Jones robbed himself," Muttonchop Ames said.

"I've given you my offhand thoughts, so I'll let you wrestle with it. That's what a crime school is for," Mugs said. "Who wishes to officiate here, before the group?"

This was going to be a joy.

No one volunteered. But then Cyrus Maguire rose. He peered around, seeing no opposition, and headed for the front of the classroom, while Mugs slipped to one side.

"I think I know who done it, but I'm not saying," Maguire began. "You all got your theories. You're all gonna spill them. I'll start with you, Smith."

"I haven't got any theories," Smith said. "What I want is to go over there and look around, but Stoopnagle's taken over. So I'll just keep my trap shut."

"No, you gotta give me a theory," Maguire said. "What kind of cop are you, anyway?"

"When was the last time the safe was open? We don't even know that," Smith said. "Mugs, when did you bring them the toy money for the heist?"

"Yesterday afternoon, before the reception here," Mugs said. "It was printed at our job printer, *The Tattler*."

"Ah, so we have more suspects. Who runs *The Tattler?*"

"Typhoid Mary. I don't know her last name and don't want to know."

"So now we have two tellers, her, and you, right?"

"Especially me," Mugs said. "I live with her, if you get the drift."

"Birdsong, you're a true pecker-head," Turk said.

"Never pay cash for anything," Mugs replied. "She was dying to print the fake bills for me. She could hardly wait. She was ready to print more than we needed. She's also printed all them Wanted Dead or Alive posters I autograph and sell. She can't stay away from me, and begs for more work."

"Mugs, you're a turd," Studebaker said.

"Anything to improve my reputation," Mugs said.

Bailey Bain stood up. "It had to be done before we even got here," he said. "Someone got into that safe and took the real bills and left the fakes. That happened before we got off the trains. Whoever did it knew that the stupid heist you staged here would cover for the real crime. And maybe throw some suspicion on us. I don't figure it's the tellers. It's Jones, and his bank was probably in trouble, and he was looking for a way out of the box."

Filibuster Smith looked annoyed. "I'm sure you got it all wrapped up, Bain," he said, a certain withering tone in his voice.

"Well, go to hell, Smith."

"Now, we'll have none of that," Maguire said. "We're going to solve this here heist and you're going to co-operate. What's your idea, Studebaker?"

"I ain't got any. If you let me talk to those tellers, and look at the safe, and figure out a few facts, maybe I'll come up with something. Meanwhile, any of you who spout ideas are simply full of shit."

"Yeah, I second that," said Manley Drake. "We're sitting on our butts in a classroom. I don't care what Stoopnagle says...let's get out there and do a job."

"He's the law," Maguire said.

"I don't give a crap," Drake said. "We're all law. Let's go."

The students all agreed, and were soon trooping toward the bank, intent on collecting a few facts before arresting anyone, or having Stoopnagle arrest anyone. A crowd had collected at the bank building, but the sheriff wasn't letting anyone in.

When the lawmen started to enter the building, Stoopnagle shouted at them to get out.

"Deputize us, Stoop," Maguire said. "Then you can give us orders we got to follow, and you got twenty lawmen working on angles you want looked at."

Stoopnagle paused, thinking about it. "I'll maybe deputize half a dozen," he said.

"I want to grill them tellers," Muttonchop Ames said. "I want to shake them till their teeth rattle."

"I've already done that," Stoopnagle said quietly. "I've known both of them for years. I know their families. I know their brothers and sisters. And I know damned well that neither of them had a thing to do with this. It's you outsiders I'm looking at. There's lawmen gone bad, happens all the time, and that's what I'm looking into. And that's why I'm not sure I want to deputize any of you."

"Don't deputize me," Mugs said. "I'm running a school."

Stoopnagle stared at him. "Especially you. In fact, you come on in here. I want to talk to you, Birdsong."

"Glad to oblige." Mugs turned to Maguire. "You're in charge. You run the crime academy while I alibi myself." Mugs laughed to beat the band.

Maguire seemed pleased with his appointment. "All right, we're going to see who or what left Rock Springs last night," he said. "We're going to talk to the post office, the express office, the livery barn, and the railroad depot."

Mugs watched Maguire take over, and then drifted into the bank, with the sheriff right behind him.

"Well, well, well," Stoopnagle said. "You show up, and we've got a heist. First bank robbery in Rock Springs. What do you say to that?"

"Gimme the third degree," Mugs said.

"Don't get smart with me, punk. You printed up that funny money you brought into this bank. You set up all this ruckus of a fake heist that wasn't. So spill the beans, and maybe you'll only do twenty at Rawlins, not thirty."

"It was all for my reputation," Mugs said. "You can't be the foremost bandit, robber, crook, killer, gunman, purse snatcher, and cherry-picker without keeping up the game."

"So, how'd you do it?"

"I wish I knew," Mugs said. "Some things are so routine I can't even remember them."

"Cut it out."

"I think maybe I've got it all stashed behind a brick wall at the orphanage, and after they let me out in ten years, I'll retire," Mugs said. "I'll go live in the Sandwich Islands. Go check brick walls for fresh mortar."

"Cut it out. Who done it?"

"Well, who could crawl into the vault?"

"That don't hold water. Things got so busy around here anyone could've."

"Anyone being the people who knew what a stack of new bills looks like?"

"You got the brains, I don't," Stoopnagle said. "Vault's open most of the time, right?"

"Do you ever get claustrophobic in bank vaults, Barney? I was trying to knock over a bank in Canada with a stand-up vault, and I got so scared the door would swing shut on me that I botched the job."

"You couldn't hardly get into this one, I guess."

"This is a big safe, Barney. A vault is built in and they import the door from Pittsburgh. I tried to get a job with the vault door company once, testing their doors, but they didn't want me, so I said how do you know it's theft proof if no one tries it out? And they said beat it. I said I'd send back results, and I did. When I knocked over the bank in Calumet, Illinois, I sent them a letter saying a drill and some nitro did it."

"Yeah, well, where'd you stash the loot this time?"

"I've bought into the moving picture business and sent it to someone named Lasky, and it should earn me a forty percent return."

"Yeah, and where's the loot, Birdsong?"

"Have you tried the express office? The post office? Maybe it got shipped to the Argentine."

"Real funny, Birdsong. I know in my bones you done it, and I'll keep after you until you cough it up or I got a witness."

"Try them tellers. I was in and outta there a lot, getting ready for the big lawman heist."

"They both got migraines. And Jones is talking about firing them."

"If the bank survives. I don't know nothing about banking, but when it's cleaned out, it's plumb dead."

"And you were the laxative," the sheriff said. He waved a bony finger. "You done it, and I'm going to get you, and I'll keep on it for twenty years if I have to, and maybe I'll nail you for something else, but you're going to pay and pay."

"Me and the Rawlins pen, we're old friends, Sheriff."

"So what's your theory?"

"I haven't got any. But it looks planned. Someone planted them fake packets in there, and that wasn't an accident. For all I know, you did it. You could walk in there and no one would slow you down."

"Birdsong, I don't know what I'm going to do with you."

"Deputize me. I'll get all those yahoos into my classroom and have them solve it, and before it's over, some of them'll be singing."

"You think they did it?"

"They heard all about the first heist. Word got around that my Academy of Crime was a hoot, and the bank lets us play the heist game. So a few of them thought that whatever's in the vault, it's better than a hundred a month sheriff salary. And they made it happen."

"I doubt it, Birdsong, but I'll listen to any crazy theory."

"Hey, I divided the class into two groups. The bank robbers were Filibuster Smith, Cyrus Maguire, Amos Turk, Muttonchop Ames, Bailey Bain, Joe Studebaker, and Marley Drake. That's the seven that started the ball rolling. That's where I'd start, if you want me to. I'll just ask the ones doing the heist what would be the best way, and I'll listen."

"Why don't I believe you?" the sheriff asked.

That's how it went the rest of the day, until Stoopnagle told him to get out of there, and not leave Rock Springs. Mugs was happy. He'd rarely been happier. He made his way back to the old orphanage and waited for all those teams of hot-shot lawmen to come in and report. He poured himself a glass of good bourbon, and chipped out a little river ice still packed in sawdust, and settled in for an entertaining day or two.

Eventually, all his students dragged in, every one of them looking baffled, frustrated, annoyed, or just plain mad. They stared dourly at Mugs, who was sitting at the front of the classroom, soaking up some good booze.

"What did you all find out from a hard day's digging?" Mugs asked.

"Not a damned thing," Cyrus Maguire said.

IX

Sheriff Stoopnagle stormed in, looking dour.

"I'm going to get to the bottom of this," he said. "Where are those sacks of fake money?"

They were both sitting in the classroom, where they had been brought by the bank robber faction of the class. The contents of each teller wicket had been dumped into a bag. A handful of the stuff had been copped by the citizens of Rock Springs.

Stoopnagle spotted the bags, and emptied one on the table, and began sorting out the fake bills.

"Well, well, well," he said, holding up a genuine one-dollar greenback.

He dug further, pulling several more out of the heap. The lawmen watched, fascinated. No one volunteered to help the sheriff. In time, the sheriff had extracted seven dollars in singles from one bag, and thirty-four real dollars, mostly ones and two-dollar greenbacks, from the other.

"Well, well, well," he said, waving the bona-fide money. "Someone got careless."

"It's a prank," Maguire said.

Stoopnagle bristled. "Right now, it's bank robbery. Where's the rest?"

"Sheriff, you're jumping the gun. Those sacks of fake money have been lying around here for days, unguarded, and anyone could have done that," Muttonchop Ames said.

"Right now, it's bank robbery," Stoopnagle said.

"It's all part of this town's big joke, Sheriff," Joe Studebaker said. "Go cool off. We're lawmen. We're not knocking over banks. We're here to learn from this here master crook how crime works."

"Well, he's a suspect and so are you. The bank's missing over eighty thousand dollars. You want to call that a joke? None of you leaves this town until this gets solved."

Mugs intervened. "Hey, you on the bank heist team, tell him how you collected the cash."

They did. They told Stoopnagle how they stormed the wickets from behind, yanked the tellers out, and emptied the cash drawers into the bag.

"It was all fake bills. That was obvious. If anyone had spotted a single dollar, that whole joke would've stopped cold," Maguire said. "Sheriff, cool down. We've got twenty lawmen here, and if the money's still in Rock Springs, we'll find it for you."

But Stoopnagle wasn't deterred. "Right now, you're all accessories. You have stolen dollars in your possession. Maybe you didn't put things in motion...I'll find that one soon...but you participated."

Mugs was enjoying the show.

"What if it's not in town? A lot of time's gone by."

Stoopnagle glowered. "Then I'll sit you down and pound it out of you."

"No one's come up with a clue," Maguire said. "We've organized into teams. We've talked to the railroad, the baggage men, the express office, and Overland Stage company, and a few teamsters. We also talked to the two livery barn people about who came and went. The money's still here. And if you'll deputize us, and authorize us to start hunting for it, we'll probably find it. One thing I know. You can't do it alone," Maguire said.

He was proving to be a good spokesman for the group.

Stoopnagle sagged. It was plain that he couldn't do it alone. His bull-headed effort to solve the crime on his own was leaking gas.

"All right," the sheriff said. "I'm not deputizing the suspects, but the rest of you stick a paw in the air and get sworn in. And that does not include you, Birdsong."

Moments later, the sheriff had thirteen new deputies.

"All right, now you'll get to work. You'll examine every outhouse vault in the city. That's a favorite way to stash loot, and we're going to make sure there's not eighty thousand dollars sitting in the bottom of a two-holer."

The newly sworn deputies looked a little dour.

"You, Billy Bob Packer, you lead a north-side team, and report to me. And you, Dangerous Dave Dellig, you tackle the south side."

"I have an outhouse allergy. I need to excuse myself for health reasons," Janos Mart said.

"You've just been undeputized," Stoopnagle said.

He pointed at the seven who were implicated by the real bills in the stash. "You seven. Your task is to prove you didn't do it. You're on your own."

"Gotcha," Maguire said, looking happy.

"And you," he said to Mugs. "You stick with me. Don't you even visit a biffy without permission."

That sounded fine to Mugs. It sure beat standing in front of some lawmen all day, trying to get them to tell stick-up stories.

The lawmen abandoned the orphanage, and set about finding the boodle. Sheriff Stoopnagle motioned, and Mugs followed. The sheriff headed straight for *The Tattler*, and corralled Typhoid Mary.

"You printed the funny money, right? Whose idea was that?"

"You're looking at him."

"How much did you print?"

"He kept wanting more. Tons of it. I ran through all my bank paper."

"What's that?"

"It's for documents, stock certificates, stuff. Hard surface. Erasers won't touch it."

"How'd he pay you?"

"He welshed. He's not man enough to pay a chippie, much less a demanding woman of art and ability and grace. He couldn't pay a knothole for services rendered."

"What do you say to that, Mugs?"

"Up yours, Typhoid."

"You mind if I look around here for the real McCoy?"

"You won't find it in Mugs's pants, Sheriff."

Sheriff Stoopnagle searched the entire shop diligently, from attic to floor, and found no loot stashed away.

"You want to interview me now for a big scoop?" he asked Typhoid.

"Big scoop of what, may I ask?"

"You are authorized to say that the sheriff, an experienced and dogged lawman and investigator, is hot on the trail of the stolen loot, and expects to recover it within the next twenty-four hours. He has more clues offered by eager citizens than any peace officer can handle, but he is reviewing each one, and already has a list of hot prospects. He expects to put the thieves behind bars shortly, and will file felony theft charges so detailed and damning that the criminals...I am revealing something here...there were three, maybe four...the criminals will cool their heels at the state pen the rest of their lives. The bank is in sound financial shape, and no citizen need fear its collapse. It will soon have its money back, except for pocket change spent by the hoods. I am also posting a fifty-dollar Reward for information leading to the arrest and conviction of the thieves. I should also add that I've eliminated about forty suspects, having determined that their alibis stood up, and they were not present at the heist or part of it. But I am working through a list of seventy-eight, some of them with records a yard long, and by the time your next issue appears, Rock Springs will be celebrating."

"In other words, you haven't a clue, you old goat."

"He has a clue," Mugs said. "He knows who the accessories are, caught them red-handed, and needs only to find the perp to solve the whole shebang."

"Perp? Perp?"

"Perpetrator, the mastermind, the arch criminal, the evil genius, who conceived and executed the heist and who has the loot safely hidden in Texas."

"You sure are vain," she said.

"He's got me fingered," Mugs said, "and he's dangling a carrot. If I show him the loot, I'm in the pen for ten, not twenty. And you can print that."

"Mugs, you're a genius," she said. "You got born with all your assets above the belt."

Typhoid Mary could be depressing, so Mugs and the sheriff bailed out of the print shop.

"Do you think she'll run the story?" Stoopnagle asked.

"Not the way you gave it to her. You gave it to her straight, and she'll blow it up big. That's how to sell newspapers. You watch...the headline will be that a hundred fifty thousand got took."

"Well, well, well," the sheriff said. "You know all about the press."

The sheriff steered them to the bank, where they found the teller cages wreathed in black crepe in honor of the heist, and a sign saying that no withdrawals over ten dollars could be done.

The sheriff ignored the tellers, pushed through the little gate, and headed for J.J. Jones, who was sipping a restorative and staring out the window upon bustling Rock Springs.

"I think I know who did it," J.J. Jones said morosely.

"Why does that make you unhappy?" Stoopnagle asked.

"Because it's a relative."

"Well, spill the beans then. We hang relatives just as well as we hang strangers."

Jones stared out the window, then eyed his visitors, and finally gathered up the courage to talk. "It was Jill Jane," he said.

That sure got Mugs's attention.

"I can't bear it, but I know it's true," the banker said.

Stoopnagle waited patiently. He knew something about confessions. But Jones was wiping away some moisture at his eyes.

"She was two-timing me. I've known about it for a while. She came here the evening ahead of the heist, opened the safe, cleaned it out, and put in the fake money."

"Ah...there must be a reason you say this," Stoopnagle said.

Jones peered up at them, and smiled wanly. "Well, I need to backtrack. I keep some rare wines in the bank safe, vintage Bordeaux, things like that. We like to serve it to guests. It's so valuable that I've kept it in the bank safe. And of course Jill Jane had the combination, so she could fetch a bottle when we were going to entertain. There's only four people who know that combination. She's one, I'm one, and the two tellers. When we discovered the packets of fake money, I also noted the wine was missing. Who'd nip that? Who even knew its value?"

He stared at his two visitors, and his voice hardened.

"It's Alabaster Seneca. The undertaker. She and Seneca have had a little party going for some while. I thought immediately that the two had plotted this miserable theft, using the carnival of the fake heist to cover their tracks. And I was right."

"How do you know? And where's the money?" the sheriff asked.

"In North Platte, Nebraska," Jones said. "I checked with the depot. A child's coffin was shipped by baggage car to North Platte that very afternoon to a funeral parlor there."

Mugs was enchanted.

"Alabaster and Jill Jane shipped the wine and the eighty thousand out, even before the shortage was discovered. And now I've discovered that Seneca is not at his place of business. And this very morning, Jill Jane vanished. I headed for the railroad station, talked to the ticket agent, and discovered that a woman of her description bought a ticket to Omaha, and boarded the morning eastbound." He sighed. "I've lost eighty thousand, my wine, and my wife."

Mugs wondered if the man was listing his losses in order of importance, and decided he was. Jill Jane was at the bottom of Jones's list.

"Well, we'll stop it," Stoopnagle said. "We'll wire the sheriff in North Platte and have him seize and return the coffin...that'll restore your cash. And I'll get warrants out on Seneca and your woman, and you'll get her back."

Jones sighed. "She's gone. She always felt I didn't meet her requirements."

"Well, this is licked. I'll let *The Tattler* know I've found the loot, and I'll be pinching the perpetrators."

"You gonna let all them lawmen off the hook?" Mugs asked.

"Of course. Salting the fake money in the teller cages with a few real bills was simply a diversion. Very clever of Seneca. Throw suspicion on some veteran lawmen, like me, to conceal his heist. Well planned, but I figured it all out, and now there's going to be some justice."

"You sure them lawmen weren't in this? A criminal ring? You sure I ain't involved? I'm a world champ crook."

"Of course I'm sure. And now I'll head for *The Tattler* to announce my success. Typhoid Mary'll whump up a good yarn."

X

In due course the disgruntled, odorous, and offended peace officers collected once again at the orphanage classroom, along with the rest, and they were all in a rebel mood.

"We looked for loot in every outhouse in the city and outside of it," said Billy Bob Packer. "We poked more crap than fits on a stick. We waited around for old people to get off the pot. You have no idea how many old people spend their days sitting in two-holers and reading Monkey Ward catalogs. Especially old men."

"It goes faster in winter, boys," Mugs said.

"We checked every privy on the south side," said Dangerous Dave Dellig. "And we came up with nothing. There's not a greenback in all that brown crap."

"Yeah, and we're supposedly paying to be educated about crime?" Packer said. "We want our money back, Birdsong. This school is a pile of manure."

"Slow down, gents, there's news. I'll tell you in a moment. But you gotta realize that this is all about the hard work of tracking down hooligans like me. You want to deal with hoods? You get up to your armpits in the brown stuff."

A distinct odor permeated the classroom. These peace officers had not escaped the inevitable consequences of their task.

"You done good," Mugs said. "You proved where the moolah isn't. By the process of elimination, we all know the greenbacks are somewhere else."

"Jaysas," said Cyrus Maguire. "Give us a refund, Birdsong. We wanna go home. Tell Stoopnagle to cut us loose. This is crap."

"Ah, my fine industrious students, here's the big news. Sheriff Stoopnagle has announced that he knows who done it, and he's putting warrants out, and these two will be arrested the moment they step off an eastbound train headed for Omaha. What's more, he's proclaimed he's recovered the loot...it has been seized by the sheriff in North Platte, Nebraska, and will be returned by express. He has already proclaimed all this to our local rag, *The Tattler*, and, if he's correct, he's bagged the whole heist and the bank will soon have its cash back. He expressly said none of you are suspected any more."

"Yeah? And who's this he's pinching?"

"He hasn't yet made a public announcement. But I know it's an inside job. Done by someone who knew the combination of the safe."

That sure got their attention.

"So what's next?" Cyrus asked.

"I believe the sheriff will soon invite you all to the unveiling, if that's how to say it, when he opens the shocking container now on its way back here, and begins to count the greenbacks, which, he says, are stuffed in there."

"Who in the bank has the combination?" Joe Studebaker asked.

"Well, he told me this much, gents. Jones the banker, two tellers, and his wife."

There was a vast sigh.

"Go wash your fingers and butts, and we will celebrate successful crime detection by the veteran peace officer, Barney Stoopnagle."

"There ain't nothing that gets this stink off me," said Dangerous Dave.

"Burn the duds. The local merchants will be pleased to sell you fresh," Mugs said. "Or visit the cathouse. They'll wash you for a fee."

"When is this unveiling?"

"When the trains come in, boy, when the whistle blows."

"I spend a whole day poking outhouse vaults, and Stoopnagle solves it standing around somewhere. Life ain't fair," said Dangerous Dave.

"That's what I like," Mugs said. "If life was fair, I'd not be a notorious criminal."

"It's the notorious part that frosts me," said Cyrus Maguire. "You got that way with advertising."

"You've got me figured out," Mugs said. "And you can take a signed Wanted dodger when you leave. It's worth something to collectors. Two dollars the item, and there's six or seven different ones for sale now."

"When does this here train come in?" Maguire asked.

"Ten-fifteen. Sheriff Stoopnagle wants us all to meet at the depot baggage room for the great unveiling. Meanwhile, you can all wine and dine."

"I never touch wine. That stuff's for sissies," said Joe Studebaker.

They all agreed to that, and drifted toward their rooms. The air began to freshen once they abandoned the classroom.

Mugs sure was enjoying himself. He could hardly wait for the great unveiling. He spent a pleasant evening gargling red-eye for his scratchy throat, while enjoying the sights in the Pink Palace, a joint directly across the street from the railroad station, and patronized by riff-raff who drifted in to see the sights.

The westbound train was twenty minutes late, but finally chuffed in and ground to a stop with a great squeal of brakes and hiss of steam, which echoed through the deep darkness. The distinguished lawmen who were attending the Academy of Crime gathered around the baggage car, along with Sheriff Stoopnagle, who had gussied himself up in a black suit, string tie, and massive

Stetson with a brim so wide it guaranteed to change the weather underneath. He sure was looking cheerful.

"Well, gents," he said. "This is the moment."

"Arrival of Train Sixty-Seven, from North Platte, Omaha, and points east," the stationmaster proclaimed. "Boarding in five minutes for Reno."

The baggage men slid open the door of the baggage car, which was immediately behind the tender, and they carefully lifted out a small coffin, diamond shaped and plain, and set it on a cart.

"That's the sucker," Stoopnagle said.

The baggage men wheeled it into the baggage room, and the assorted lawmen gathered around. They were none too sober, having drowned a day of mucking crap with spirits and steaks. But they were ready. They knew this would be an impressive moment. The sheriff would shine. At the last, the bank president himself, J.J. Jones, appeared, dressed in his best funeral suit and cravat, with polished high-top shoes. He allowed a few swift smiles, but they were mixed with sadness.

Stoopnagle had a few hand tools ready for action, and discovered that the lid had been screwed down. So he calmly turned the screws loose, one by one, in the light of two kerosene lamps, which cast a buttery light over the solemn proceedings.

Ten screws in all, which he diligently removed, while the crowd watched silently.

"All right," he said. "The perpetrator of the heist is the town's undertaker, Alabaster Seneca, in cahoots with Mister Jones's estranged wife, who had the combination to the safe, and made the switch in advance of the theatrics of the next day. They are being pinched when they step off the train in Omaha just about now, and will be returned here for trial."

The lawmen were impressed. "Good job, Barney," said Filibuster Smith.

Stoopnagle wiggled the lid loose, and lifted, and they all stared in.

There lay a little boy with an enormous, elongated head, attached to a withered little body, dressed in blue. There was nothing else. No false bottom, no compartments, no cloth lining. A faint malodor arose from the box.

Stoopnagle slowly deflated, and then slid the lid back on, and motioned to the baggage men. "Close it up and return it," he said.

The lawmen watched silently, none of them venturing an opinion. They had all been prepared to buy the sheriff a drink. Stoopnagle turned away from them, and drifted into the evening, and was soon gone from sight. Mugs felt sorry for him. He rarely felt sorry for anyone, but old Stoopnagle was worthy of a little pity.

"Well, gents, it's not over," Mugs said. "Maybe Mister Jones, here, will explain."

Jones looked unhappy, but finally summoned his courage. "There is reason to believe my estranged wife, along with the undertaker, planned and executed a defalcation. We'll know in due course."

"What's that mean?" Mugs asked.

"A misappropriation," the banker said, looking pained. "Good evening." The man, struggling to stand upright, walked into the night.

"Wyoming gonna extradite those two?" one of the lawmen asked.

"Beats me," Mugs said.

And that's how the evening ended.

The next day Mugs led his class through the basics of jewel theft, cat burglary, stick-ups, and forgery. Then he dealt with confidence men and crooked madams.

"I got advanced degrees in the whole lot," he said.

But late in the afternoon, an astonishing thing happened. Old Stoopnagle walked in, along with Jill Jane Jones and Alabaster Seneca.

"The trip to Omaha was not flight...they bought round-trip tickets, fully intending to return this afternoon," Stoopnagle said. "They were not parties to the bank robbery."

"Then why'd they go to Omaha?" Mugs asked, reflecting the curiosity of the whole class.

"To establish grounds for a divorce," Stoopnagle said. "Missus Jones wishes to be freed from Mister Jones, and a trip with her gentleman friend was called for."

That was a turn of events, all right.

"We sure had a fine time, Alabaster and me," Jill Jane said. She was looking a little smirky. "My husband is not a manly man. I'm sure the judge will understand."

That explained everything, at least to some of her auditors.

"So, have you any leads?" Maguire asked.

"No, and I'd welcome any help from you fellas. You know your stuff...I don't seem to."

"Who was the little boy?" Maguire asked.

"Poor child. Little Pearl Perkins, born with one of those big heads and little torsos. Survived four years and was gone. Most pitiable," Seneca said. "Sent to be buried alongside his maternal grandparents. His parents grieve."

"Who do you think nabbed the bank money?" Filibuster Smith asked the couple.

"I doubt that anyone will ever know," Jill Jane said.

"All right, gents, go solve the crime," Mugs said. "Far as I know, you're still deputized by Sheriff Stoopnagle, and there's a big heist that needs your attention. The sheriff is a little indisposed, so it's up to you. You get an A in course work if you nip the perp...a D-minus if you blow it. That won't look so good on your records, now will it?"

"You got any ideas. Mugs, you old crook?"

"Shake the locals until they rattle," Mugs said. "Make the canary sing."

"You're a big help, Mugs," said Amos Turk, who normally was the most silent of that bunch. But the rest were itching to start in, and all had a shiny deputy commission giving them some muscle. If twenty fine lawmen couldn't figure it out, no one could.

Twenty experienced lawmen spread out through Rock Springs that day. They interviewed the tellers and Jones. They studied the safe and its contents. They checked the saloons for big spenders. They checked the stores for big spenders. They had little visits with engineers and firemen, wondering if any had been paid to deliver a satchel somewhere. They looked into bank records, wanting to know if Jones's bank was in trouble before the heist. They dug up the receipt for the delivery of cash from the Treasury.

As the days wore on, they began to doubt whether they'd ever figure this one out.

"This'll pop open someday, maybe not soon, but someone who's got eighty grand is going to spend it, and it'll be noticed, or he'll try again, and get caught," said Maguire, who had become an unofficial spokesman for the bunch.

"I still think Jill Jane had a hand in it," said Filibuster Smith. "No one's cleared her...she had a motive, to embarrass her husband. One place we haven't searched is Jones's own house and carriage barn. There's an icehouse, too, and a root cellar. And the trash heap back there."

With Jones's reluctant permission, they raided his own house, surprising Jill Jane, and searched relentlessly, even in the rafters of the carriage barn. All of that yielded nothing.

And then the course came to an end.

"Gents, ya done a good job, good as anyone could do," Mugs said. "You're all getting a B-minus, and this here diploma saying you're a master of criminal detection from the Mugs Birdsong Academy of Crime, Rock Springs, Wyoming."

XI

Mugs settled into great quietness, awaiting the next class in a few weeks. He took an interest in costume jewelry, especially the hobbyist variety. He wanted to learn how to make it, and where to get the stuff. A catalog issued by a Kansas City outfit offered what he needed, and soon he had a lot of junk, including jeweler's tools and a tiny bench vise, and lots of baubles, all sent to Harry Karpov, general delivery, Rock Springs.

He debated whether to pursue Jill Jane Jones, since it turned out she was already stolen by Seneca, and he wouldn't get much satisfaction out of stealing her from someone who didn't want her. That was a disappointment. But he still wanted to add wife-stealing to his criminal record, and thought that stealing her would be good practice, and he'd learn a few things about copping wives if he gave her a whirl.

The bank had settled back into grudging business, with very little cash on hand, but it seemed to survive somehow. Jones was testy, and no longer welcomed him. And of course there would be no more gaudy bank robberies to celebrate the opening day of his crime school courses. It would all be theoretical stuff in classrooms from now on, and no practical experience knocking over banks or trains.

So one chill day he knocked on the Jones door, and was met by Jill Jane herself.

"You," she said. "I'm disappointed in you. I was expecting a real wife-stealer, and you haven't shown up for weeks."

"I've been learning a new trade," he said. "And I wasn't sure there would be anything in it for me, now that you've been stolen by the undertaker."

"Oh, him. I just used him so J.J., my dear old poobah, could go to court and get a divorce. Adultery's the one thing that works, you know."

"Yeah, well, if you want to get stolen, come by the orphanage this evening."

"That sounds like an invitation," she said.

She knocked on his orphanage suite about seven that evening and he let her in. She was wearing a gorgeous translucent summer frock, which buttoned down its front and looked about right for burglary.

"Little booze, little wine?" he asked.

"Wine's for sissies. Lay some real stuff on this old gal, you old crook, and don't cheat."

He poured her some bourbon and added a little pond ice he had purloined from a sawdust-lined icehouse he discovered on the north side of town.

"Old Jones still keeping you under lock and key?" he asked.

"The poor old pooh. He knows he's not a manly man, and he knows I'm a wild mare, but he's not interested in getting rid of me. He sort of wants me around."

Mugs sipped a tiny bit of the booze, but he had watered it down because he needed to stay nimble.

The evening proceeded handsomely. Mugs told her that the next class might even include some famous lawmen who were handier with firearms than he would ever be. She told him that her dear old hubby was grouchy, drank hot chocolate each evening, and went to bed at eight-thirty, and she was bored stiff.

He poured a couple more, and she smiled a lot, and he judged the time was ripe, so he fixed her one with a Mickey Finn, and she sipped it.

"Oh!" she said, smiled, and passed out.

That was perfect. He stretched her out on the sofa, worked the wedding ring off her finger, and examined it. The ring had a one-carat blue sparkler, which couldn't be better. He set up his little jeweler's workshop, with the tiny vise clamped to a table, and anchored the ring in it. Then he carefully pried up the prongs, released the superb blue diamond, removed it, and dug around in his box of glass baubles until he found just the right stone. With a little wiggling and working, he slid it into place, and then pressed the clamps down. When he was finished, the ring looked very like it did before, except the stone was glass. It would probably be a long time before she discovered the switcheroo. He slid it onto her bony finger, jammed the purloined diamond into a tin of chewing tobacco, and put away all his costume jewelry supplies and equipment.

He had to wait a while for her to come around. It was getting late, and she was annoying, but he had to finish the rosy scenario. Eventually she did stir, her eyes opened, she beheld Mugs, and groaned.

"I drank a little more than I intended," she said.

"That's all right, Jill Jane."

She stared at her clothing. "Why didn't you take advantage of me?"

"I'm too tired," he said.

"I knew you'd disappoint me," she said.

That's how the evening ended. She vanished into the night. He felt happy. Nipping a diamond was far better than wife-stealing, and likely to go undiscovered for years. There was a whole future in it. With a little refining of techniques, he could live on easy street the rest of his days. He hit the sack a happy man.

But was awakened early in the morning by an ominous knocking on the orphanage door. He discovered Sheriff Stoopnagle there, bristling with importance. But the sheriff also was carrying a large black leather Gladstone bag.

"Well, well, well," the sheriff said, and let himself in.

"The bag addressed to Charles Zinfandel, Principality of Monaco, got as far as New York and got sent back here. It lacked transit papers. And guess what? I rifled the lock, and guess what? Eighty thousand in nice new Treasury notes. And guess what? Nobody around here is named Zinfandel. There's not a bottle of it in Rock Springs, and I had to ask Charley, the barkeep, what it was. White wine. Trouble is, I don't know who sent it. Well, I know, but I can't prove a damned thing. No one saw you nip it and ship it. But the shipping tag was out of sequence. It was an older tag...newer tags have higher numbers. So here we are, Birdsong. I've been thinking real hard about it."

"You can actually think?" Mugs asked.

"Here's the scoop, Birdsong. Everything in Rock Springs is real quiet until you arrive and start up your school. Then the peace got disturbed. And the bank got robbed. Now, I'm not saying you done it, but I'm saying that I'm shutting down this here crime college. It's done. It's over. You got twenty-four hours to close her up and get out of Rock Springs."

"Fine with me," Mugs said. "Kind of a desperate place, nothing but rock around here, and not a good saloon. Lots of men in overalls. You got a good reason to shut down my school?"

"I don't need a reason," Stoopnagle said. "I'm shutting it down without any reason at all. Go hire a lawyer if you don't like it."

"Well, I'll pursue another occupation," Mugs said. "I liked teaching, but it's hard work. I have an aversion to work. I want life to flow by easily. Maybe I'll move to Los Angeles."

"Wherever," Stoopnagle said. "Just do it now."

"You on your way to J.J. Jones? Mind if I come along?"

"Suit yourself."

They hiked to the bank, where Jones was busy rearranging furniture in the lobby.

"Well, well, well," said Stoopnagle. He handed the Gladstone to Jones, who peered in, lifted a packet of twenties, a packet of fifties, and then began whipping out packets of greenbacks in great number.

"Eighty grand," Stoopnagle said. "I counted it. All yours. How's that for law enforcement?"

Jones smiled, and then sighed. "Jill Jane did it, you know. Omaha was only the first stop. They were off to the French Riviera. Now I'll have to change the combination on the safe. Sheriff, you're a gem. Oh, what a glorious day in Rock Springs, the most sublime city in the United States."

"Yeah, well, we're going to get rid of Birdsong here, and shut down his crime school. No more trouble in Rock Springs."

"That's a pity. He's been an outstanding citizen and help, and the school has improved the economy."

"Yeah, I'm a diamond in the rough," Birdsong said.

"What are your plans, Birdsong?"

"The contemplative life, J.J. I'm heading for a Trappist monastery in upstate New York. I'm in debt to the universe, and I need to make amends."

"I'll let Jill Jane know. She's rather fond of you."

They shook on it.

"Twenty-four hours," said Stoopnagle. "Or you're off to Rawlins."

Mugs headed for *The Tattler*, and found Typhoid Mary breaking up old pages.

"I hate this," she said. "Breaking down old type's not my idea of a good life. Look at me, full of ink. A life of stained fingers."

"Yeah, well, I need to borrow a lot of money," Mugs said.

"For what? You got the bank loot. Don't tell me otherwise."

"Nah, the sheriff's got it, and he's returning it to Jones. Say, that's a scoop. You've got a story. Sheriff Recovers Loot."

"How'd he get it?"

"He'll tell you all about it. In fact, you'll hear more about it than you want to hear. He'll come in here and talk your ear off. He's booted me out of Rock Springs. I've thanked the saints and angels for it. But I got no place to go."

"Where would you like to go?"

"Oh, the French Riviera. I'm thinking about the Principality of Monaco, and becoming a jewel thief. I've been working on a foolproof way to nip the ice. I gave it a spin, and it works fine, so that's my plan, and there's more jewels on the Riviera than anywhere else, so my life is finally coming together. But I still need a ticket."

"What am I gonna do with all these signed Wanted posters if you leave?"

"You gonna spot me the cash or not?"

"I'm tired of setting type and breaking it down. I'm tired of Rock Springs. It's desert. I want ocean. I'm going with you. I'm outta this place."

"You? The Riviera?"

"Hell yes, Mugs. Let's go. You'll get a ticket, but only if I get a ticket, too."

* * * * *

The final issue of *The Tattler* reported that Sheriff Stoopnagle had recovered the booty stolen from the bank. The sheriff suspected that it was an inside job, and was gathering evidence. J.J. Jones, the bank's president, said his bank was sound and back in business and ready to make new loans at only slightly usurious rates. Sheriff Stoopnagle announced that the Mugs Birdsong Academy of Crime had shut its doors, and its proprietor was leaving. The sheriff was honoring Mugs Birdsong at a banquet for his outstanding contributions to the criminal justice system. And that this would be the final issue of *The Tattler*. Its editor was moving abroad.

THE SQUARE REPORTER

Crafty Jim Fair wanted some puffery. They all do. There's not a mine operator in Virginia City who couldn't use some publicity when he wants to jack up the price of the shares. That's when they come to me.

He knew where to scout me. My crystal chandeliered editorial offices are at the Old Magnolia, hard by *The Territorial Enterprise*. I am rarely in the newspaper plant itself. It is the privilege of seniority to issue my copy from my own venue.

I am William Wright, and I scribble the mining news in between various feature items and obituaries, so the mining magnates seek me out, along with my colleagues at rival sheets. We mining reporters are a privileged lot. Nowhere else on earth do millionaires and nabobs come, hat in hand, looking for a favor. They especially come to me because I accept no bribes, unlike certain fellows at other papers, so my services are cheap.

It's a game we play: they want to use us for nefarious purposes, and we reporters like to lounge around with flat pilsner in hand and tell each other how virtuous and broke we are, and how we value the loftier things in life and scorn the filthy lucre, except, of course, whenever we can get our mitts on some. But it is true that I own no mining stocks, and the world knows it.

After much contemplation, I have concluded that my success is due to my disparate parts. I am half Quaker and half cynic. By design I live a bachelor life in this liveliest and loosest metropolis of the West, while sending greenbacks now and then, mostly then, to my dear wife Caroline and five sprouts in West Liberty, Iowa.

They sought years ago to join me here, but I resist. This is no town for innocents. If I, a true devotee of the Society of Friends, occasionally fall into a saloon brawl and joyously bloody my knuckles, against all my instincts and spiritual inclination, what hope is there for my stainless boys? So, to spare them temptation and a world of vices, I keep them in Iowa.

Now everyone agrees that it is impossible for a cynic and a Quaker to coexist inside the same skull, but I manage to reconcile the two at the mahogany bar of Old Magnolia. I begin my reconciliation about ten every morning, and by midafternoon I am fully reconciled and at peace with the world.

Jim Fair knew exactly when to catch me properly reconciled, and therefore arrived at two-thirty, bought me additional reconciliation to demonstrate his bona-fides, allowed me one of his spastic crocodile smiles, which employ unaccustomed muscles, and turned at once to business.

"Old friend, we're turning up some pretty good silver sulphides, and I thought you might want to do a little story," he said.

Old friend indeed. For Jim Fair, "old friend" was an oxymoron. But this was progress. Fair and his shamrock partners, Mackay, Flood, and O'Brien, had kept a tight lid on their diggings, and anyone snooping around was likely to get smacked with a shillelagh. They had found some decent silver ore, that was clear enough. I heard they were buying up neighboring mines, especially the California and Ophir, but that had been tough to pin down.

"I might," I allowed, edging my empty tumbler outward, but Fair didn't bite.

"You go in there, old friend, take all the samples you want, no one will job you. We're at the twelve-hundred-foot level and ore's getting richer the deeper we go. Get your samples assayed and write her up."

I allowed as I would, and nudged my forlorn glass another inch Fairward, but he ignored me, studying the fat nude over the backbar. When it comes to drinks, there is nothing worse than an Irish Protestant.

I knew what this was all about. Mine supervisors actually mine the shareholders better than they mine ore, a fact little understood outside of certain gaudy circles on the Comstock, and this was a managerial attempt to jack up the stock. At any rate, I would be the first reporter down the Con Virginia shaft since the Irish scooped up the place, and that was story enough.

I collected my pick hammer, a tape measure, and a samples bag, and headed for the Consolidated Virginia shaft, where a double-decker cage dropped me from bright afternoon into the hot dark, foul-aired confines of their works. They were sure busy down there, drifting into promising ore and running cross-cuts to see the width of the lode.

I'm an old hand in mines, unlike some of the gross cowards who report the mining news from up on grass, like that kid Clemens who used to hang around this sinful burg. So I was looking not just for ore, but for country rock, diabase, porphyry, the stuff not worth a nickel that had to be hauled out, too, the stuff that wipes out profits.

I peered about, my carbide lamp throwing livid light on the glistening black silver ore, took the measurement of the drift, some two hundred feet in all, and the width of the cross-cuts, thirty to forty feet, which were impressive. Then I chipped off six samples I considered typical, while all about me sweating miners mucked and timbered and laid rail. No one jobbed me; no one steered me away from any area. I took my finds to an independent assayer I could bribe with *Enterprise* expense money, and just for good measure went back the next day and took two more samples and gave them to another assayer.

The results raised my brows. The four Irishmen had found a large body of good ore, not the highest grade by any means, but enough to put lace doilies on their armchairs. The first six samples averaged three hundred and seventy-nine dollars to the ton, and the other two samples averaged four hundred and forty-three.

I thought they were on to something. The *Enterprise* headlines said it all:

CONSOLIDATED VIRGINIA

A LOOK THROUGH THE LONG FORBIDDEN LOWER LEVELS
THE ORE BODIES AND BREASTS, WINZES AND DRIFTS
RICH DEVELOPMENTS

I suppose Jim Fair thought that would inflate his Con Virginia stock, but I got the last laugh. The shares rose all right, from a flat fifty dollars to fifty and a quarter, and there they hovered weeks on end. The speculators had already priced his bonanza and yawned at my news.

Beetle-browed Rollin Daggett, editor of the *Enterprise*, chuckled along with me. When the mood was upon him, he shifted his editorial office to the Old Magnolia and edited the paper with a carafe of Steamboat Gin ever before him, sipping and scribbling, lipping Havanas and bellowing for a copy boy.

"They'll be back," Daggett said. "Soon as they figure out a new way to con their investors, they'll try again."

We drank to that. I intended to ask him for a five a month raise, but needed a good peg to hang it on. The moment had not arrived, but I kept waiting for an opening. He knew I was going to ask, so we circled each other like sumo wrestlers.

I turned to my other occupation, which was writing outrage. The world mostly knows me as Dan DeQuille, because that's the by-line I use. The object of the game we scribes all play in Virginia City is to spin a whopper, and do so with such sobriety and earnestness that we sucker the whole subscriber list, most of California, and half the exchange papers on the other side of the globe into believing every word. It's a modest talent of mine, but not one that gets me raises.

I had in mind a little spoof, and set out to write the sad story of one inventor named Jonathan Newhouse, who contrived a suit of solar armor with which to cross Death Valley in the hellish heat of day. Within the armor, Newhouse wore a thick layer of sponge, and he artfully arranged that this sponge could be refreshed with water now and then from a portable reservoir strapped to his back. The water evaporating from the sponge would cool down Newhouse. Newhouse set forth, confident that he was proof against the terrors of Death Valley, and so it seemed. But alas, water evaporated so fast in Death Valley that poor Newhouse froze to death. He was discovered sitting upright, a block of ice, the victim of his own genius.

I published that assay into science and technology and sat back, and ere long the *London Daily Telegraph* solemnly reported in its news columns the strange case of an inventor in far-off Nevada who had developed a suit of solar armor and had frozen to death inside of it.

Oh, we had fun with that. Daggett even bought me a carafe of rye, a thing unheard of in the long and sordid history of Daggettry. It was only later, when the rye was gone, that I sadly realized he had craftily derailed my request for a raise.

I had a rival at this racket for a while, an edgy redhead named Sam Clemens, who tried his hand at the hoax business, didn't do badly, but lacked my touch. His literary efforts always seemed to have a target or two in mind because he was a mean piece of work.

After Clemens had hovered around the *Enterprise* for a couple of years, he wrote an item that managed to offend all seven virtuous women in Virginia City, was promptly challenged to a duel, and was advised by the city's impeccable authorities to make himself scarce within twenty-four hours or face the nasty consequences. He vamoosed for San Francisco, hung around there for a while, and then headed for other and warmer climates, unsatisfied with life as it is lived in the Far West, which is hard on the sensitive and neurasthenic.

Since then I've had no contender in the hoax department, and I rather yearn for a rival just to keep myself fit. Most people would suppose it is the cynic in me that produces these inventive stories, and the Quaker part of me that yields the fair and square mining news. But that would be just wrong. Only a true Friend, filled with Inner Light and an innocent spirit, could pen a piece that required absolute solemnity and earnestness. No, the cynic in me covers the mining news, for only a cynic could cope with the machinations and absquatulations of the stock jobbers and mine-salters and bonanza-manufacturers who populate every street corner of Virginia City.

Meanwhile, the four lucky Irishmen had not been idle. Sitting atop a modest fortune inspires one to purchase the neighboring lots, so they expanded their holdings in all directions, especially the Ophir next door, even while burrowing ever deeper into the hot wet stone of the Comstock. I kept abreast of this, mostly by nefarious means known to all reporters, namely bribing the miners for information and smuggled ore samples, and paying stock brokers for tips. For the Con Virginia was once again sealed off from inquiring eyes, and that flint-lipped manager, Jim Fair, was death on the press.

What an odd lot those four sons of Erin were. Fair, squinty and suspicious, the type who cuts wages and blames the cut on his partners. John Mackay, gymnast and boxer, affable and generous, an empire builder. James Flood, who ran the San Francisco end of the operation, shrewdly buying and selling the company's stock. And William O'Brien, the most exalted of the lot, a former resort keeper, company errand boy, inclined to buy drinks for cronies and lose money at poker.

They were the best thing Virginia City had going, since most of the other great mines like the Gould and Curry were playing out, working low-grade ore and losing money.

One thing I knew for sure: the Irish were digging deeper than anyone else on the Comstock, and the deeper into that hot rock they pierced, the better the ore, and the wider the lode. I published my small mining items in the *Enterprise*, sent a little pay back to West Liberty with admonitions to enjoy the wholesome climate and steady life of Iowa, and roved the resorts of the Comstock with such reprobates as I could collect for an evening's entertainment.

The day came, however, when I was summoned once again into the august presence of Jim Fair, who, if anything, had gotten craftier and meaner in the succeeding months.

"Go on in there and write her up again, DeQuille. No one will job you. Go where you want. Tell the whole bloomin' world what you see. You got sharp eyes. You're the one reporter what can do the job right."

That was the first compliment ever known to issue from Fair's lips, and it took me an hour to get over the shock and paralysis of it. I knew he wanted something in return, but it was still a watershed. In two years, he had bought me three drinks in all, accompanied by six requests for one story or another, which came to half a drink per pleading. I knew him for the most successful mine manager on the Comstock, and his ways were plain: buy cheap, sell dear. I had been bought with a compliment.

I took note of the stock prices in San Francisco before descending that January of 1875. Fair and his cronies had managed to jack the price of Con Virginia and California and Ophir to record heights by gulling poor Philipp Deidesheimer, legendary mining engineer and *authority*, into announcing right out in public that the bonanza was worth a billion and a half simoleons. I wondered what Fair had poured into that bewildered man's lager.

In any case, the market value of the shares of the three bonanza mines exceeded the value of all the real estate in San Francisco, which says a thing about wily Jim Fair and his cronies. I supposed that the Irish were going for broke, and might soon own California unless they were planning to buy Ireland, which is why they summoned me, a lowly Quaker in Virginia City, to deliver the *coup de grace*.

So, down I went in my felt hat and jumper, this time riding the first three-decker cage on the Comstock, into the black bowels of the bonanza, and stepped off at the fifteen-hundred-foot level. Sample bag and pick hammer in hand, I edged into a fairyland, a long gallery supported by timbers and dotted by twinkling lights in every direction where hundreds of sweating and bare-chested men hacked at the ore. I was assaulted by a roar, as man and machine scooped and chipped and smashed rock with a mad frenzy.

Here was the bonanza. These miners weren't drifting along a six-inch seam; they were entirely *inside* the seam. Cross-cuts every hundred feet showed that the ore ran far to either side. There was a fair amount of porphyry mixed in; this wasn't solid silver and gold ore, but there was more of the black stuff than these eyes had beheld in one glance ever before; more than I ever imagined I would see again, more than the whole world had ever seen in one place. What's more, shafts and winzes revealed ore from the twelve-hundred-foot level down to the sixteen-fifty.

Here was a body of ore that staggered the mind, turned pastry chefs and chambermaids into Midases, threatened to swamp the monetary system. I wandered about in a daze, my mind refusing to accept what my senses reported. I chipped samples out of the gallery at various levels, more from each of the cross-cuts. My hands trembled so much I banged my thumb, and my fingers refused to guide my pencil. Then I took out my tape measure to put some footage into my calculations. I thought to myself, I could walk out of here with a thousand dollars in my pockets.

Shaken, I ascended to grass in the battered cage, gathered my wits, put an assayer to work on my samples, and began my calculation. I finally concluded, after ruining half a pad of newsprint, that the ore in sight down there, which ranged from nine hundred dollars a ton down to eighty, was worth over one hundred and sixteen million dollars, and that was just what I saw with my own eyes. I published my findings on January 5, 1875, and the result was entertaining to watch.

San Francisco went mad. People emptied their bank accounts and bought any Comstock shares, at any price. Even the four Irishmen went mad and bought their own stock, which begat even more madness. Brokers couldn't keep up. Banks shuttered their windows for lack of funds. People gathered in the streets to exchange tips and rumors. Some lucky stiffs whumped up fortunes overnight, getting filthy rich with one buy-and-sell. San Francisco sprouted multimillionaires as if they were cabbages. People did dizzy waltzes and jigs on the street, and tipped bellboys with silver dollars.

It didn't last. The smarter pencil-pushers studied my story, soon realized the mines had been overbought, so they began selling. Then it all came rumbling down. Brokers called in the margin accounts. Millionaires joined breadlines, butlers were selling apples, and banks quaked on their foundations. A few hundred million paper dollars vanished in hours. Actually, the bonanza mines didn't fare badly; the lucky Irish came out fine. But every shopgirl in San Francisco along with the rest of the nation had been had.

I watched all this with a certain Quakerish delight. My bonanza story had gotten a better play than any of my hoaxes. And virtue had triumphed. Fair had wanted me to jack up stock prices that were already grotesque, and I had pulled the plug instead. Old Virginia City was the same as ever; it was California that had been wrung out and hung up to dry.

I took to writing sketches for the *Enterprise*, and dabbling with literary masterpieces, and no erstwhile millionaire ever wandered into the Magnolia and threatened to put me six feet under.

One fine spring eve Daggett lumbered into the Old Magnolia and arrayed himself at his accustomed spot at the rear. A carafe of Steamboat appeared, along with the appurtenances, which he handled with all the ritual and reverence of a priest, sipping and aahhing. In time, he summoned me with a nod of his shaggy head.

"Well, you did it," he said. "Because of you, nations wobble, millionaires are washing dishes, and Bible-thumpers are smug, and that's the worst of it."

"It's a strange thing," I said. "I walked into that hole at the Con Virginia and before my eyes was the biggest pot of silver and gold in all recorded history, more than most men can even imagine, more than their wildest dreams. But it wasn't enough. Their greed had already ballooned it ten times over, and when they absorbed the truth, their dreams died. They never even understood the wonder of it."

"You have regrets?" he asked, one eyebrow cocked.

"For what?"

"You could have made a killing. You could have five butlers and a masseuse. Own the *Enterprise*. You could bathe in gin."

"Oh, that. No, Rollin, I did my duty. I'm a square reporter, right down to the garters. I own not one mining share, I'm influenced by no man, write nothing but the facts, and buy and sell nothing but words.... It was a good story."

He nodded and sipped the Steamboat, whistled sonorously through his crooked teeth. "Yes, we newsmen have other and loftier pursuits," he said, eyeing me. "We are a noble lot. Morally superior."

"Without a doubt. For me, a good true story, a scoop, a light thrown on darkness, is worth more than all the millions those greedy rascals ever heaped up. It's not filthy lucre that motivates a man like me."

"I'm glad to hear it, Dan," he said. "Now I won't have to give you a raise."

THE LAST DAYS OF
DOMINIC PRINCE

This is about a rancher named Dominic Prince whose family had run scrub cattle in a remote desert waste of southern Arizona ever since God kicked Adam and Eve out of Eden. It's about a man who believed in the eternal verities: that people would always eat beef, that ranching was good, that cattlemen embodied an old and honored tradition in America.

And this is also about people with other ideas: that ranchers rape the good earth, destroy the environment, fatten at the federal trough, put saturated fats on our tables, and kill any beast that competes for forage with their livestock. And it is about the way the world changed in the Sixties and Seventies, and how a lot of people began to celebrate nature and the environment, and how they got caught up in the push to preserve what was left of the natural world.

But before I get too deep into all that, I have to tell you how I got to know Prince. I'm an Easterner, an advertising account executive with a big Lexington Avenue agency. So you would not expect me to know anyone like Prince or to live in a remote corner of Arizona as far from civilization as I could get.

But I had come to that place for healing, having wrecked my marriage and career and damaged my reputation so spectacularly that erstwhile friends just shook their heads. I won't go into all that. This is about Prince, not me. I'll say only that I fled New York after the divorce, quit my position — or was I pushed out? — and ventured into the Arizona wilderness to put my life in order. I had read Joseph Wood Krutch's *The Voice of the Desert*, and believed that healing might come from the desert. That was where prophets listened to God.

That's how I met Dominic. I drifted down to Sasabe, a sun-baked burg on the Mexican border, sixty miles of dirt road southwest of Tucson, looking for a place to acquire some wisdom for half a year or so. I ended up renting an adobe tin-roofed house squatting next to a windmill and mesquite corrals seventeen miles from the Sasabe road. It was grim, simple, stark, and ugly.

There, surrounded by rocky wastes, cholla, ocotillo, yucca, and stately saguaro cactus, I tried to mend myself and shake the city from my bones. Eventually I probed deep into the cholla-choked cañons of his ranch, alone under the relentless sun, my mind dwelling long on virtue and vice, sin and love, ambition and despair.

When I first drove out to Dominic's ranch, along gritty clay roads guarded by rattlers and Gila monsters, I wondered what would happen when I asked to rent his empty adobe. I supposed he would just laugh at an urban man who was going to play cowboy a few months.

But Dominic was a larger man than that. He heard me out, agreed on a rental price of one hundred a month, and I moved in, along with a load of junk furniture from Tucson. When I bought an old dude-string horse and tack from a neighboring guest ranch, he extended the same courtesy, and if he was amused by a greenhorn fooling around with a gentle nag, he never let on.

Dominic's image is etched in my mind even now, three decades later. He never slouched, but stood bandy-legged and straight up, with innate dignity. His face had been stained the color of a chestnut by the ruthless sun, his eyes bleached of color and webbed by squinting. I discovered later that his family was Majorcan, but had been in the United States virtually from his birth.

"I have a man living in that little 'dobe out at the corrals," he said. "His name is José, and he don't speak English. He's Mexican and works by the month. He goes home the end of each month for a couple of days. He'll be no trouble."

That surprised me. Dominic didn't say so, but I suspected the whole deal was illegal, and that proved to be correct. I wondered how that could be, why the Border Patrol didn't clamp down. They had to know about José; their ubiquitous green four-wheel vehicles prowled that country night and day. But Dominic had his *vaquero*, and no one stopped him.

Later, after I had sunk some roots into the Altar Valley, I fashioned an explanation. That remote valley was a major conduit for marijuana and harder stuff coming up from Mexico. The feds needed the co-operation of local ranchers, who acted as their eyes and ears, to keep a lid on that traffic. I realized there might be an unspoken *quid pro quo*: if the ranchers helped the feds, the feds would not look very closely at the ranch help.

José received his pay in precious dollars at the end of each month, and then he would vanish from the little 'dobe behind my house, riding through the night back to Mexico, which he entered through an ordinary wire ranch gate far from the port of Sasabe. Dominic told me later that if José was being conscientious, he would fork over about ten bucks to his *esposa* for food for herself and the *niños* before heading for the nearest *cantina* and setting up the *cervezas* until he had blown the whole wad.

But sometimes he forgot to give something to his wife, and then the family would starve for a month, subsisting on simple fare, rice and pinto beans, drawn from great burlap sacks, until the next pay day. If José failed to return for work after a few days, Dominic would drive across the line in his old rattletrap and tell José it was time to report at the ranch.

And then I would wake up and discover José's ratty pony in the corral, and sometimes mesquite smoke drifting from the stovepipe of his 'dobe shack. All these comings and goings would occur at night, hidden from the cyclops eye of the Border Patrol units and aircraft.

Dominic visited almost daily, and I got to enjoy the sound of his clanking Ford pickup truck grinding up the slope to the old adobe. His truck had a rattle for every occasion, and sometimes rattled just for the fun of it. I can't imagine what taciturn old Dominic saw in me for a friend, and once I suspected he was keeping an eye on me for the feds, but that soon passed. We talked ranching, and sometimes Dominic invited me for a truck ride down wild and precarious two-rut trails that dropped into cañons, crawled up ocotillo-choked slopes, and burst into little green Edens where a few cottonwoods or palo verde had poked roots into moisture.

He usually brought with him a .25-caliber automatic, and I wondered why. It wasn't the weapon of choice for killing a rattle-snake or destroying a wounded cow. It lay loose on the bench seat of his pickup. When I began to patrol his ranch with him, the thing made me nervous because it inevitably bounced around until its barrel was aimed at my buttocks. I wasn't exactly relaxed when a loaded pistol in a careening truck was threatening to turn me into a soprano. On those occasions, I delicately fingered the little firearm around until I was out of the line of fire. Dominic caught me at it once, smiled, and stuffed it into the crack between the seat and its back. We never saw a soul, neither a drug runner nor a harmless "wet", as the locals called an illegal immigrant. But that little shooter was Dominic's ace if he needed one.

Dominic was suffering hard times, but I gathered that most ranchers always suffer hard times. On a Sonora Desert ranch, there are good bad times, and bad bad times, and, once in a generation, some bad good times. But never good good times.

"I'm tired of subsidizin' the beef-eatin' public," he said at least once every time we met. He knew plenty about ranching, at least the old-style variety. He ran no blooded cows, got much of his young stock from Mexico, and pastured it until it was ready for fattening at a feedlot. These ribby little Mexican *corrientes*, as common cattle were called, were admirably adapted to make a living in a harsh desert, and prospered where fancier cattle sickened or starved.

Occasionally he imported the *corrientes* through the Sasabe port, and those crossings were always festive occasions largely orchestrated by federal officials. The bawling, skinny, bug-eyed, multicolored, long-horned cattle were avalanched from Mexican semis by *vaqueros* with cattle prods, inspected by Agriculture Department veterinarians while still south of the border, and then forced to swim through vile-smelling sheep dip that massacred every varmint in the hides of the bony beasts. The stuff usually massacred a few cows, too, whose heads were poked deep into the brew to exterminate bugs in their ears. It didn't take much of that stuff in a cow's lung to kill it, and Dominic always figured on losing a few head.

There were usually endless and mysterious delays, and more federal officials than cowboys and truck drivers, but somehow the job always got done and semis drove the *corrientes* up to Dominic's spread, and the cowboys got down to the *cerveza* in the *cantinas*.

Thus it had always been, and always would be, as far as Dominic was concerned. But the world was changing. Dominic was almost unaware of it, living as he did in one of the most remote corners of the United States. Sometimes change burrowed into his hide like a screwworm fly. Every time he spotted a long-haired flower child wandering through Sasabe like some tropical orchid, he growled.

"Hippie," was his universal epithet. In his mind that was a fine and handsome substitute for all the derisions anyone had ever visited upon anyone else up until the year of our Lord 1972.

"Those damned hippies have never worked a day in their life," he'd say, skimming meaning out of it.

"Those damned hippies just want to shut down the world."

"Those damned hippies prefer rattlesnakes to beef."

"Those damned hippies...."

That was Dominic's litany.

I passed muster because I wore my hair short, never wore sandals, once held a high-paying job, believed in marriage, didn't despise soldiers, didn't burn flags and brassieres, had no use for Che Guevara, and didn't sound as though I wanted to harvest sugarcane in Cuba alongside the *campesinos*.

I don't really know what Dominic believed, or whether he had thought much about life. I once probed gently, wanting to know if he loved the Sonora Desert the way I did. I was ravished by its harsh beauty, its prickly flora, its brooding silence, its voluptuous blooms, its murderous reptiles, and its sheer grandeur. Not far to the north, the blue bread-loaf mass of Baboquivari loomed mysteriously, a sullen stairway to God, ready to inspire mystics. I don't think Dominic ever gave it a thought.

The more I probed Dominic's vast *rancho*, the more I awakened to the ways the silent thorny desert hid its treasures. In many a hidden arroyo the remains of a settlement endured: a tumbled-down mesquite corral, a caved-in adobe or two, and usually a few yellow-clay graves, some protected by black wrought-iron, others by weathered picket fences that had endured the sun a hundred years, but almost all without markers. The graves were all Mexican. They are a race very good at dying. And in every case, the fierce Sonora Desert had defeated the hopes and dreams of those who spun out their painful lives in those remote cañons. Each of those *estancias* filled me with great tenderness.

I loved the desert because of its beauty and mystery. I suspected that Dominic didn't love it at all, except as a home, and as the devil he knew rather than the devil he didn't know. When I told him how beautiful that vast, blistered, rocky land seemed to me, and how like a prayer, he turned silent.

It was a hard land populated by hungry people. José used a hunk of threadbare carpet as a saddle blanket, systematically grinding fistulas into the withers of Dominic's good ranch horses. Surely that was because he was so poor, I thought. I was horrified at the ruin of good horses, so I bought José a thick blue saddle pad, gave it to him as a *regalo*, gift, and thought I had preserved a good animal or two.

But the next day he again saddled up a ranch horse with the threadbare carpet. My saddle pad hung on the wall of his adobe. There it remained until his monthly excursion south of the line, and then it disappeared into Mexico, never to be seen by my eyes again. It probably bought him a dozen *cervezas*. There was more than poverty at work in all that.

Life on that border endured, unchanged, preoccupied with the only thing that counted in a harsh desert: survival.

That's how it went until one autumnal dusk, when Dominic and José were riding back to the ranch headquarters after a hard day vaccinating cattle. Something caught Dominic's eye. There, scarcely more than ten yards distant, crouched a mountain lion, frozen in place and watching the riders approach.

Dominic told me later: "I didn't even think about it. I just saw that big cat, built a loop, and let go. It settled right over that lion's neck, and I dallied up and backed my horse. I had a lion on my line."

He told it casually, as if this were an everyday occurrence, rather than the first time on earth that a cowman had lassoed a mountain lion. But it was not a casual event.

The lion sprang away until the rope flipped him, and then turned on his tormentor. In two graceful bounds, it leaped straight at the panicked horse, and sailed just over the mane, its claws flailing murderously. It landed on the other side, turned and crouched to leap again, fighting the rope, even as Dominic fought his berserk gelding. But José had not been idle. Expertly he built his own loop and sailed it under the cat's haunches and yanked it tight. Swiftly the two horses backed until the ropes were taut. Dominic and José had the seething mountain line headed and heeled, stretched between the two ropes by crazed horses, but no less dangerous for that.

Dominic slipped off his skittery saddle horse, found a stout piece of mesquite, and gingerly approached the raging lion. He brained the cat repeatedly until it died.

Shaking and distrustful, they surveyed their prize: an adult male puma, stretching around six feet in length not including its tail, a tawny gray color, perfect and unmarked.

It took some doing to load the lion onto the back of the saddler, which snorted and shied, but Dominic quieted the nag and led it back to the ranch house.

I didn't know about if for a day or two, but when I stopped by his house to pay the rent, he led me to his chest-type freezer and opened it. There, stretched across a bed of white-packaged beef, lay a lion so magnificent I could not have imagined a more perfect specimen.

"My God, Dominic!"

"He's big for a lion."

"Tell me about him!"

He grinned and shrugged. I had a tough time getting him to tell his story. He didn't want it known, and would just as soon have hidden it from the world ever more.

"What are you going to do?" I asked.

"I don't know. No taxidermist'll touch it without a tag."

So there the lion lay, in frozen magnificence. But the story didn't freeze, and soon it was whispered about the Altar Valley that Dominic Prince and his *vaquero* José had roped a mountain lion and lived to tell about it.

Stockmen quietly assured their listeners that never in the history of the world had such a thing ever happened. Prince had been catapulted into that mysterious realm of legend and myth. He had become the world's ultimate cowman, the John Wayne of all ranching people, a man of such courage and skill that he had triumphed over the most dangerous beast of the desert.

As for Dominic, he grew even more taciturn, deflecting questions or admiring comments with a slight grin. But I knew he was enjoying every moment of it.

"Better keep it quiet," he said. "Next thing I know, they'll want to fine me for it. And take away my lion."

As the days slid by, I brooded about that cat in his freezer and wondered what its fate would be. I didn't learn until weeks later, when he invited me into his spacious ranch home and showed me the exquisitely tanned lion pelt on the waxed plank floor in front of the fireplace, its jaws open, its saber teeth menacing, its yellow glass eyes peering up at me, its velvety pelt shading from dove gray along the spine to warm earth tones on the flanks, its claws no less menacing on the planks than in life.

"It's a flat six feet, butt to nose," he said proudly.

"How'd you do that?" I asked.

"Smuggled it down to Hermosillo."

"Ah! I didn't know they had taxidermists down there."

He looked pained. The things a New Yorker didn't know would fill several books. "Better than ours," he said.

"How'd you get him back?"

"Smuggled him in a heap of burlap bags. And don't you say nothing."

That made sense. No one at the port ever pawed through the rat's nest in the bed of his rattletrap truck.

He had even recovered the thick mesquite limb that had battered the cat to death, and now it stood beside his fireplace. I knew at once that all this loomed bright and shining in his mind; this was a feat unheard of, the very reason he had been set upon this earth. He had tenderly gathered the pelt and club and placed them at his hearth, the place of honor. Someday someone would spin a ballad about Dominic Prince and his mountain lion.

About José's role in all this, Dominic remained silent. He did not want the story to reach the ears of U.S. Immigration people, though I don't doubt they heard all about it within hours of the event.

José was more loquacious, and the story swiftly burgeoned through Sonora. Whenever Dominic slipped across the line to buy cattle or stop for some *cerveza*, he received a hero's welcome. Who could imagine such a thing? José was a hero. Dominic was a hero. What sort of *hombre* was this *gringo*?

That should have been the end of the story, but it was only the beginning. A tale like that won't die, so it crept outward like ripples on a pond, and the *Tucson Citizen* got wind of it.

A reporter called Dominic: Was it true?

Dominic, a man with a sophisticated knowledge of the border, but little knowledge of the press, reluctantly owned to it, and the paper published the amazing story of the only man ever to rope a mountain lion and live. I saw these things unfold, bit by bit, and surmised that there would be more chapters.

I knew I could not tarry much longer in the desert, even though I had come to love it. I had to earn a living, and in advertising employment is much like musical chairs. If I didn't get back into it soon, I probably never would.

Things returned to normal. Dominic stopped by for coffee, and the rattle of his old Ford was my cue to put on a fresh pot. He never spoke of the lion. I told him what the desert had done for me and what I hoped to take from the desert to New York. I especially wanted to take with me my newfound sense of sovereignty. In the desert, each man is a king.

In that lonely place I had read history, hiked, ridden my horse and listened to the voices of the land, and the prophets, and my heart. I had begun to make my own decisions, set my own goals, establish my own values, and armor myself, as the cactus did, against the world. I knew I would be a stronger man when I went back East, better able to love and give and work.

But this is not about me; it's about Dominic.

One day he sat down with me, toyed with his java, squinted,

and announced that some woman from Johnny Carson's staff had phoned him: Was it true? Would he be willing to talk about it on national TV? Would he be agreeable to a preliminary interview?

I saw the flesh around Dominic's eyes crinkle with amusement.

"I guess I will," he said. "It ain't a secret."

And off he went to New York.

They treated him graciously on the Carson show. I drove into town to watch it at the *cantina*. There he was, a bandy-legged rancher in a new, stiff pearl-gray Western suit, his face and hands the color of old saddles, responding reluctantly but firmly to each of Carson's questions. There, before a nationwide audience, Dominic told about roping, heading and heeling the lion, and putting the great feline in his freezer. They liked that in New York. They don't see ranchers very often in the Big Apple, much less lion-ropers.

I pretty well guessed what was coming, but I kept quiet. Dominic returned, spent a day or two enjoying his life as a local celebrity, settled back to work — and then the mail came.

Not a few letters, but heavy canvas sacks full of mail, delivered by the unhappy rural delivery man. Dominic stared, amazed, at the mounting pile of them, and summoned me to find out what to do with them. He couldn't imagine responding to all those people, and I assured him he didn't have to.

I had a hunch, born of years in advertising and public relations, that Dominic wasn't going to enjoy most of these, and I warned him:

"You know, Dom, the world's changing."

"Hippies," he growled.

"Yes, and animal-rights people and environmentalists."

He just growled, deep in his throat.

I wondered where his wife had vanished to. I scarcely had met her, even though I had dropped by his ranch house many times. She apparently had divided the world into men's and women's business, and made herself scarce when she thought she didn't belong.

"Well, how do you want to do it?" I asked.

"Just read a few. I'm no good with handwritin'."

"Sure," I said, pulling a fistful of envelopes from one of the gray canvas sacks.

I slit one open and what I saw, in a woman's hand, didn't encourage me to read.

"Well, ah...."

Dominic settled into a dining chair and wrapped himself in silence.

"Ah, she says...

'I saw you on Johnny Carson, and all I can say is you're the meanest man I ever met. What had that lion done to you? Nothing. But you just had to kill it to prove what a he-man you are. Now the world has one less beautiful lion....'"

I eyed Dominic, who sat resolutely, revealing nothing.

I tried the next one:

Don't you realize, sir, that lions are an endangered species, and that if they are killed off by thoughtless people like you, for no reason at all, the world will not only be an emptier and uglier place, but the life cycle will be disturbed....

Dominic sat like a Sphinx.

I pulled a scented blue sheet from an envelope:

There you go, raping the environment, just the way all ranchers do. You just can't stand to let any natural creature live, can you? You just have to show how big and tough you are, and before we know it, there won't be anything left on earth except your filthy cattle....

I looked at Dominic. Tough he might well be, but at five-feet seven or so, he was scarcely big. His face remained expressionless.

I tore open another:

Well, now you have your reputation and you can strut around and be a big-time rancher. But the lion you killed for no valid reason was helping to keep nature in balance. Predators are vital to the whole cycle of life. Why did you do it? A real man, loving and sensitive, would not have even dreamed of such a vicious act.

Dominic looked stoic.

I read a bunch more that evening, twenty or thirty in all, scarcely a dent in that pile of letters. At least in that bunch, not a letter praised him, and the tone ranged from hostile to vicious.

"That's enough," he said, although the evening was young.

"Do you want me to read these and sort them, pro and con?"

He stared into the darkness. "I've heard enough," he said.

"You mind if I look at a few hundred?"

He shrugged. I took that for acceptance, and loaded a sack into my truck.

I spent a couple of days working through them. Most people expressed outrage, contempt, and an innate hostility toward ranchers, who they stereotyped as dumb, greedy, ruthless, and parasitical. Most contained finger-wagging lessons in ecology, garnered from the media. A few did admire Dominic. To a handful he was awesome. Some messages were mixed, extolling his bravery and daring, yet scolding him for his destruction of a beautiful and proud animal.

I drove over to his place a few evenings later and reported my findings: in that batch, three hundred eighty-seven hostile, thirty-seven mixed, four favorable. Most attacked him on ecological grounds. A smaller number assailed him for cruelty. A large number described ranching and ranchers as rapists of the land, and they used terms so spiteful they shocked me. The whole world, it seemed, had landed on Dominic.

"It doesn't matter," he said.

There was something about the way he said it that awakened

my concern. In the space of a few days, Dominic had aged. He slumped now instead of standing erect. Instead of listening quietly, and joining in conversation, his mind seemed to drift to horizons unknown to me.

It did matter.

I spent my last weeks in the desert trying to buck him up, but he simply shrank deeper and deeper into himself, and began to let his ranch slide. Before, when José would linger south of the line too long, Dominic would go roust him out. Now he just drove his dirt roads and looked at his skinny little *corrientes* and did nothing.

I tried to fathom what was eating Dominic. I thought he would shrug off all the hostile mail. He had been tough and independent all his life; what difference did a bunch of angry letters make? He could go on living exactly as before...but that wasn't the way his life was spinning out now. It was as if four thousand angry letters had broken his spirit, even though he had read only the smallest fraction of them. The things people believed about ranchers hurt him.

"They don't know where their food comes from," he muttered one day. "Let 'em try starvin'."

That's how it went my last weeks in the desert, and when I finally packed up for New York, I could see he was still slipping day by day. A man can carry only so much hatred on his shoulders.

Then I said good-bye. I drove over to his place to leave the key and tell him and his wife I was on my way, and to thank them for the desert interlude that had renewed me.

"Dominic, I've enjoyed every minute of it. You've taught me about life. You're good company...."

I fumbled through the parting, and finally drove away, haunted by the dullness in Dominic's eyes, and the slouch of his body, and, above all, by the walls of silence surrounding him.

I did not like New York as much as I once did, even though I landed a new position at a fatter wage than before. Dominic gradually slipped from mind, and over the next year my sojourn in Arizona became an abstraction. New York was real; the Sonora Desert and its people, and Dominic Prince, had faded.

And then I received news of his death — a printed announcement on a card mailed by his family. And I knew that four thousand angry letters had become too much for any man to carry on his shoulders.

I grieved, and wished I knew how to keep the world from changing so fast.

DEAD WEIGHT

> HERE LIES THE COFFIN-MAKER
> BARCELONA BROWN
> LAID IN HIS FINEST,
> SIX FEET DOWN

Dodge City does a good deal of dying, which is good for business. Mostly it's a summer occupation, when the drovers push up from Texas with their longhorns and beeline for the saloons with some Yankee dollars in their jeans. They tend to perforate one another after downing a few tumblers of red-eye.

We get a little help from hot weather complaints as well, such as dysentery and cholera, and sometimes the ague. There is not much business in the winter, with the Texians gone south like the geese, but sometimes a consumptive parts from us when a good Canadian blue norther cuts through, or the catarrh or lung fever swathes through town, and then Doc McCarty ends up recommending me, Phineas Agnew, to the bereaved. McCarty and I try to steal each other's business, but in the end I always win. Morticians have a monopoly. It isn't a perfect monopoly, because sometimes there is no *corpus delicti*. But it's good enough for a man wanting a secure living, without the vagaries of boom and bust, famine or plenty.

I always come out ahead. It's an art, you see. To maximize the profit, you have to catch them at just the right moment. The moment of deepest grief is the time to suggest the finest casket, the fanciest send-off. When those Texians come up the long trail carrying one of their own in the cavvy wagon, all swathed in canvas, killed by lightning south of town or a stampede or bad water, then's when I mint money.

Surely, I say, you would each expect the same from your comrades of the long trail? Surely your dear old mothers would want the finest money could buy? Surely you want to do better than the Bar X, or the Hashknife boys, who bought a princely box for their departed? Surely, after all that suffering on the long trail, the lonely nights, the endless rains, the dismal food, you want to provide some comfort for your friend? A fine, waterproof, spacious, oak coffin, and a dandy parade, with a coronet band playing dirges and my four-horse black lacquered equipage with cut-glass windows and black pom-poms to take the departed to his last home?

That always works, and as fast as their trail boss shells out the trail wages, they're appropriating the fanciest box they can afford for old Tom or Red or Dusty, and forking over cartwheels for all the extras, too.

It is a principle of my business to sell the gaudiest goods just when the widow is wiping back the first flood of tears, or when the children, bereft, orphaned, adrift, are suddenly faced with the loss of their pa or ma, or maybe even a grandmother or aunt.

Now, I don't keep many coffins on the shelf because it isn't necessary, or at least it wasn't until recently. Dodge City was blessed with a cabinetmaker of uncommon ability, able to do magical things with wood. I had only to call upon Barcelona Brown for whatever I needed, and within hours he would have a splendid box ready for me, and for a modest price, too, which often enabled me to charge triple or quadruple the tariff, depending on who I was dealing with. A new widow would sometimes count out five or six times the price and be glad of it, certain she was doing her wifeliest for her deceased spouse, who succumbed to a buggy wreck.

I have always been aware that my business requires a certain political delicacy. I have been stalwart for strict enforcement of gun laws north of the deadline, that is, the Santa Fe track cleaving the town, even though there are certain popular watering holes north of the divide on Front Street, such as the Long Branch and the Alamo.

But south of the deadline is another pasture. I have always opposed rigorous law enforcement in that quaint quarter because it is bad for business. If the Texians wish to get into shooting affrays, that shines up my profits, and I hardly see why Mayor Dog Kelley and the muckety-mucks should concern themselves with it. The cowboys are expendable Texians, not Kansans. Often, I have declaimed to assorted deaf lawmen about that very thing. For example, I've braced Ford County Sheriff Bat Masterson several times, and Deputy City Marshal Wyatt Earp as well, suggesting a policy of liberality south of the deadline.

But I digress. My real vocation here is to tell about the coffin-maker Barcelona Brown, and explain his odd fate. I called the fellow the wizard of wood. He was a skinny, dreamy bachelor with wire-rimmed spectacles and a sniffle, and if he ever thought of acquiring a spouse, I never had an inkling of it. He was wedded to wood, if you will forgive that odd perception. Brown could conjure up a box so swiftly I could not fathom how he managed it. He thought of caskets the way kings think of palaces. A proper coffin should match the character and status of the departed, and be a comfort to the bereaved. An ideal coffin should impart glory, laud, and honor upon the bones within.

I shall always remember Barcelona Brown for the odd duck he was; the only man on earth so absorbed with the making of coffins that he could think of little else. It was a vocation even more sacred to him than a monk's. During those long stretches when his talents were not called upon, he sank into melancholia, and built gaudy furniture with a morose passivity that drove some customers away. He was in great demand to furnish bordellos, which wanted flameproof nightstands and sturdy double-reinforced beds, as well as elaborate parlor appurtenances. This he would do in a detached and wooden manner, for his heart was in coffins.

Normally, on that matter he didn't deal with the public at all. I would ascertain what the bereaved desired, whether a plain rectangular box, or a diamond-shaped coffin that apexed at the chest and narrowed at the foot, or a showy affair with nickel furnishings, and, lo, he would set aside all other work in his board and batten white-washed shop on Chestnut Street, west of the business district, and produce the item.

Thus he acquired a reputation. Anyone in Ford County who knew anything about send-offs, wanted a Barcelona Brown box. They knew they were getting the best of the art, with the wood so keenly joined that not a particle of light burrowed through any crack, the corners so perfectly mitered that the pieces of wood seemed to become one. He plainly guarded his trade secrets, and discouraged onlookers, so that he could proceed to build his boxes all alone, under the triple-lamp work light depended over his bench.

He was cranky about wood, constantly haranguing Eastern suppliers to send him only the smoothest-grained oak and ash and hickory or walnut. Each of his boxes was a masterpiece of joining, but also an artistic creation as well, the wood so perfectly and harmoniously blending or contrasting, depending on the style, that people laid hand to it to verify that their eyes hadn't deceived them.

Fortunately, Dodge straddled the Santa Fe Railroad, which enabled Brown to order materials from afar, even though the metropolis lay beyond the frontier, and was barely past its rude beginnings. The express cars regularly disgorged exotic wood on his account.

He began to line his coffins with various fabrics, sometimes black velvet, other times water-shot white silk, or gray taffeta, all carefully sewn and glued into place. But then he decided that one's eternal rest should be comfortable, and he began buying goose down from a Slovakian farmer's widow north of town, and contracting out the manufacture of quilted liners to the various seamstresses.

"Seems to me the departed should ought to be treated right, Phineas," he announced to me on one occasion, when I had hurried over to order a plain pine planter beefed up to endure a trip back to Texas. A cattleman had died of corruption in the Dodge House, of corruption of the liver, and his crew wanted to take him home to the banks of the Pedernales.

"Just a strong pine box, sealed so they won't have to endure the odors. That's what they want."

Barcelona had shaken his head. "A cattleman ought to be laid out proper," he said. "I can do what they want, but you had ought to tell them that the man deserves more respect."

Irritably, Brown had set to work, and when I called that evening, he was putting the final touches on the box. Pine it may have been under the enamel, but now it gleamed blackly in the lamplight. It boasted fine filigreed nickel handles, and a strong black lid lined with felt, and a gray silk interior.

"Now don't you go hammering the lid down," Brown had said. "You got to screw it down tight so it'll never come up or leak."

I had promised I would, and the next dawn, when the crew rode up to carry their boss home, I presented them with a pine box such as they had never before seen.

"Your late captain. He's in there, and he'll have an easy passage. Now, this here is watertighter than a brandy bottle, and you can float Mister Roberts across the rivers in a pinch, but I don't recommend it," I said.

"That's some box," the foreman said.

"Finest made, by Dodge's own Barcelona Brown. Now, that's

two hundred eighty-nine for the coffin, and a hundred twenty for my professional services."

"That's a lot for a pine box."

"That's no pine box, son, that's a Barcelona, the Tiffany of coffin-makers."

"More than we wanted."

"It's what you got. Now, do I receive the honest fruits of my labor so that I can release the departed to your tender care?"

They eyed the coffin, wonderment in their sun-blasted faces. Brown had outdone himself. This was a coffin that would promote a senator.

"Sort of fits the old man," one allowed.

They paid. Company funds, of course.

One day I happened into Brown's tidy woodworking works and discovered him in an uncommonly cheerful mood. He had, scattered about, various pieces of costly ebony, obviously from different species of the tree: some of it was jet black, the variety found in Ceylon and India, others a warmer black, found in Niger, and then there was a stack of precious Calamander of Africa, the hazel brown wood mottled or striped with black. I knew something about ebony. It comes from the heartwood of the ebony tree. The rest of the trunk is a perfectly ordinary color.

"Phineas, I'm going to make me the lord of all caskets," he whispered as he shaved a glowing black board with a drawknife. "I have in mind parking it in your window, right there on Front Street, for all the world to witness. Guess it should bring you some business."

"I, ah, we'll wait and see," I said, not wanting to commit to anything like that.

It took him a fortnight to construct it, and when I next saw it, he was nearly done. The box glowed malevolently. It was diamond-shaped and exceptionally long. Its walls consisted of three courses of ebony: brown-black at the top and bottom, jet black in the middle, all joined so seamlessly that they seemed a single piece of wood. The interior had been lined with lead sheeting, carefully soldered at every joint to foil moisture, and somehow wedded to the wood. Royal blue water-shot silk quilting lined the interior, and the north end sported a pillow, also of royal blue.

The cover, which he was still polishing, was shaped from the Calamander, and arched triumphantly over the box. A blank brass nameplate had been screwed into it.

"It's entirely watertight, once it's sealed," he said. "The lead, you know."

"It looks awfully heavy, Barcelona."

"It is. It's the heaviest coffin ever made. But look...I've added handles."

Sure enough, five ornate silver-plated handles graced each side, enabling ten pallbearers to shoulder the coffin.

"It sure is a comfort. I wouldn't mind spending eternity in it myself," he said. "Fact is, I've been sleeping in it, just to try it out."

He promptly undid his apron, stepped onto a stool, slipped into the coffin, and laid his hands across his breast, eyes closed. Then, after a long ticking moment, he sat upright, smiling, and eased out, being careful not to blemish his masterwork. He had the strangest, dreamiest look on his skinny face, a look such as I had never before witnessed on the face of the living, though I struggle hard to achieve just such an expression for the viewing of the departed.

That struck me as distinctly peculiar, but I said nothing.

"Done tomorrow," he said. "I'd sure like to put it in your window."

I decided it would attract business. There's nothing like death to open the purse strings. Citizens would gape. A few would come in and inquire. The truth of it was, there was no other casket on earth that even approached this one. They buried kings of France in less. No ancient pharaoh, wrapped in his mummy windings, got to rest in a tomb like that one.

"All right, bring it over."

"I'll need some stevedores."

"I'll find them," I said. "What price shall I ask for it?"

"Oh, it's not for sale, Phineas."

"Then what is the object?"

"I have made the perfect coffin. Let the world see it."

"How about a two-thousand-dollar price?"

He stared sourly at me, his Adam's apple bobbing up and down. "That is obscene," he said.

"Three thousand, then."

"You don't understand. It's a work of art." He just shook his head at me as if I were a dunce.

"I will take bids," I said. "Some cattleman will want it. Either that or a madam. I imagine there are harlots hereabout who'd pay whatever you ask."

But he had turned his back to me, fondly rubbing the gleaming ebony with an oiled rag that smelled of lacquer.

I planned to force the issue: money talks. Hand him five hundred dollars in gold eagles and he would wilt fast enough. Then I would sell it for six times the investment.

I waited all the next day, but got no word from Brown that he had completed work on his masterpiece. Obviously, he was adding filigrees, or maybe inlaying some exotic wood, or parqueting the lid, or carving a lion in bas-relief into the glowing ebony.

I understood. A Rembrandt of coffin-making would not stop until he had perfected his coffin. He did not summon me that day, nor the next.

That afternoon, Deputy City Marshal Wyatt Earp wandered in, as he or another of the constables often did. It was understood in Dodge that anything found in the pockets of the deceased belonged in the public till to establish city parks, and I ended up with a little pickle jar wherein I deposited silver and gold and base metal coin and bills and rings and fillings found on the late lamented. I carefully did not inquire as to the ultimate disposition of that material, but I noted that it never appeared in the town budget.

"Phineas, what's the matter with Brown?" he asked gently, supposing I would know.

I stared at him blankly.

Deputy Earp sighed. "Last night he headed for the Lady Gay and proceeded to get into a fight with three Texians, with painful results. The brawl trumped Eddie Foy for a few minutes."

"Painful?"

"Doc McCarty had to sew up his flesh here and there and splint a finger. What got into him?"

"You suppose, just because we are allied in serving the bereaved, that I know anything about him," I said. "In fact, I know very little. He's a vast mystery to me. He bachelors alone, lives and breathes woodworking, smells like varnish, has no known friends, though I call myself one, and eats solitary meals at Beatty and Kelley's restaurant, tips waitresses extravagantly, and attends the Union Church on occasion, always placing a dime in the collection plate."

"You got no idea what got into him? I'm inclined not to haul him before the JP. Let it go."

I shook my head. "Just what happened?" I asked.

"Brown was on the prod. Like he itched to start a fight. Them Texians, they took one look at the skinny fellow and just laughed it off. Lots of witnesses to that."

"Then?"

"He called one of them Texians, gent named Clay Allison, a son of a whore."

"And?"

"He took umbrage. Can't say as I blame him. But Brown should know better. Allison isn't one to call any name but mister. Anyhow, I'm gonna sort of put Brown under your care. He's not going anywhere for a few days. Hope you don't need a coffin before then."

"I can put the deceased on ice."

I concluded it was just a quirk. Barcelona Brown would soon be back at his bench, cutting and joining precious hardwoods into fine coffins, or making chairs when the body business was slack.

It took a week. Then one day Barcelona was back in his shop, sporting some purple and yellow bruises and bandaged hands, but at least he was working again. I didn't bring up the issue, thinking that whatever had planted the bur under his saddle had long since vanished.

But I was wrong.

About the time the purple and yellow began to fade from his hands and face, Barcelona decided to do some gambling. Now, the man had never gambled in his life, as far as I know. But gamble he did, one memorable evening, in the Lady Gay. Naïf that he was, he settled down at the green baize table that hid the south half of Ben Thompson, who was not only a ruthless gambler but also renowned for his ability to conclude arguments by perforation.

I was counting on Thompson to supply me with the major part of my trade that summer, but I guess Marshal Larry Deger or Assistant Marshal Ed Masterson or maybe even Earp warned him that he would be disinvited from Dodge if he got too fractious. And so far he had behaved himself, much to my sorrow, as it was a slow summer and I had anticipated much more custom.

At any rate, Barcelona Brown bought into a five-card stud poker game, lost steadily, fidgeted in his chair, imbibed ardent spirits, eyed the comely serving wenches, and surrendered a considerable sum. According to witnesses, Brown suddenly sat upright in his chair and called Thompson a cheat.

I've heard it from a dozen sources. They all agreed that the Lady Gay turned so silent that they could hear Dora Hand singing sweetly in the *Comique* at the rear, and everyone agreed that half the habitués of that spa began termiting through the cracks, including four other sports at that table.

And all agree that Thompson pushed back the rim of his bowler, his gestures cat-like and dangerous, and then laughed shortly, baring yellow teeth.

"Beat it, farmer," he said softly. Farmer was the worst epithet in the sporting vocabulary.

"I called you a cheat." Brown sat there, rigid.

"Vamoose."

About then Ed Masterson got wind of it, clapped his dainty paw on Barcelona, lifted him bodily from his chair, and propelled him through the batwing doors.

It was a wonder. Never before had dapper Ben Thompson shown forbearance under such circumstances. The town talked of nothing else for three days.

But I had begun to fathom what lay behind this sudden shift in Barcelona's conduct. Could it be? Yes, it had to be. I resolved to talk the young man out of such ghastly nonsense, and if need be, provide such company as a man adrift needs to anchor himself back in the world.

I braced him most sincerely the very next day, my black stovepipe hat in hand. He was serenely planing a walnut plank as I addressed him.

"Barcelona, my friend, how could you? Your motive is perfectly transparent. But you ignore certain realities. It is not sleep that transpires in a coffin, but eternal nothingness. You may indeed fashion a perfect bed for someone suffering lumbago, but it avails naught the person whose soul has fled.

"You may indeed wish to be buried in the finest casket ever fashioned, but do it in good time, after a life well spent. Not now. The world needs the finest cabinetmaker and coffin builder alive, and if you go, your gifts go with you.

"Plainly you are suffering the melancholia, and I intend to shepherd you until this season has passed. It is a sacrifice, of course, because I would otherwise have your custom, or that of your estate, but I am setting all that aside for the sake of friendship. Let me hear no more of these trips to the edge of the River Styx."

He smiled and nodded, and I supposed that my little lecture had its intended effect. At least I heard no more of reckless conduct on the part of my coffin-maker. He settled back into his routine, shaping and shaving wood, and yielding up masterworks of furniture, cabinets, and coffins.

All this while, that magnificent coffin lay atop two sawhorses in his shop, waiting to swallow bones. He never talked about it and, as far as I could tell, never thought to do anything more about it. I presumed that whatever had seized him had passed, and eventually it would sell just as the rest of his coffins had sold, but for a premium. Indeed, when I was making certain arrangements with Rose Dwyer, who lay in fatal decline on her four-poster surrounded by her nymphs of the prairie, I confided to her that I knew of a coffin that would surpass any other on earth, and that for a considerable sum I thought its maker might part with it.

She took the matter under advisement, but died before coming to any decision, and I buried her in a mahogany box with gold-plated handles, having supplied a bugle corps and honor guard from Fort Dodge. She said she had been in the service of her country and wanted a military burial. I knew she had at least been in the service of Fort Dodge, but didn't wish to dispute the issue. That was a particularly profitable occasion.

I did not neglect my commitment to Brown, and took him out on occasion. We went to see Fannie Garretson at the *Comique*, and Barcelona allowed as how her flesh resembled good birch. And we saw Eddy Foy at Ham Bell's Varieties, and Barcelona opined that the comic's flaying arms reminded him of a drop-leaf table.

"I think you should cultivate a woman," I said one night.

"That would be nice," he replied.

"You might find a proper one at the Union Church."

"I've noticed one there, shiny as an oak pew," he said.

I took that for progress.

Then one day, when the cattle shipping season was fading,

Barcelona delivered a small box while I was rouging the lips of a departed child. He stared at the small still body and sighed.

"I've been thinking, it's time to bring that coffin over to put in your window for a public viewing," he said.

"Well, fine. I'll get my equipage harnessed up, and maybe we can empty out the Alamo Saloon to help lift it."

"You won't need the hearse. I've calculated the weight very carefully. Just bring ten men and we'll carry it. Meet me at six."

I took him at his word, and at a quarter to the hour, I entered the Alamo and announced that there would be free lagers for ten gents who would help carry an empty coffin from Brown's shop to my establishment.

That won a cadre and in due course we converged on the shop, lifted the coffin under the watchful eye of Barcelona, and carried it through the streets of Dodge to its next resting place, behind the plate glass window of my establishment, which I had prepared by draping two sawhorses in black velvet.

"That's some coffin. Heavy as sin. Who's it for?" one of the Alamo's barflies asked.

"It's not for sale," Barcelona replied loftily. "It is the culmination of my art."

"Me, all I need is a winding sheet, a wake, and a bottle in me hand," the gent said.

The remark was distasteful. I paid off the pallbearers with a silver dollar, which could be tendered for ten draft beers, thanked them, and determined to deduct the dollar from Barcelona's next invoice.

We watched the gents troop back to the Alamo. It was late and I wished to close up for the night.

"That coffin will attract attention tomorrow," I said. "It is a phenomenon."

"I brought a sign," Barcelona said.

He handed me a hand-printed placard that explained the coffin to passers-by. I read it swiftly in the dying light, just to make sure its dignity was in keeping with my standards. It was. It simply announced that this coffin, made of three varieties of ebony, was the masterwork of Barcelona Brown. It had a quilted navy blue silk interior, lead lining, and was absolutely water and airtight when the lid was screwed down. And it was not for sale.

"You really should put a price on it, Barcelona," I said. "Even a fancy price. Maybe three thousand. Who knows?"

He shook his head. "Not for sale, not ever."

"Well, what will we do with it?"

"Just display it. And keep it closed."

I agreed, and he walked off into the darkness of my meeting hall. I heard the front door click. He probably wanted his supper. I turned down the wick until the lamp blued out, returned the lamp to my workbench, and abandoned the establishment, locking the door with my skeleton key.

The next day was routine. Several people did stop by and admire the coffin, and all of them wanted to know the price.

"Ask Brown," I said. "I'd put a two-thousand-dollar tag on it myself."

"Two thousand? That's a fortune!"

"There'll never be another like it," I replied.

Two days later I walked over to Brown's shop, intending to order a coffin for a drover who had been decapitated falling off a wagon and under a wheel.

The place was dark and cold. "Barcelona, where are you?" I yelled, but I was just talking to myself.

I tried three more times, but the man was elsewhere. I knew he wouldn't go far, not with his prized coffin two blocks away.

I tried again the next day, and found him not at his bench. Uneasily I tried his room above the Odd Fellows Hall and found no one present. I finally realized that the constables ought to be told, so I alerted the city marshal, Larry Deger, and mentioned it to Ed Masterson, too. They looked the town over, even peering into the vault of the outhouse behind his shop, and could not find Brown.

Then over oysters that night it came to me. I summoned the marshals and we headed for my establishment, where I lit a kerosene lamp and carried it to the front window.

"I think he's in there," I said.

Deger looked at Masterson, and both looked at me. None of us wanted to open that lid. But finally I did, slowly. A fetid odor smacked me at once.

Barcelona was in there, all right, still intact but a bit ripe.

Masterson sighed. "It figures," he muttered.

"I'll have the coroner look him over," Deger said. "After that, he's yours."

"I'll bill the estate," I said.

A COMMERCIAL PROPOSITION

The pox was steaming up the river. I heard it while dealing, which is how I get my news. Some passengers aboard the *Walter B. Dance* had it, and the captain intended to unload them at Fort Benton, along with his cargo. That's all anyone knew. And we would not have known that but for the horseman who arrived ahead of the stern-wheeler.

At first I welcomed the proposition. A good round of smallpox would clear Fort Benton of all those vermin-ridden Blackfeet skulking around, and the whole town would be better for it. The redskins were peculiarly vulnerable to the pox, and died in a magnificent hurry. White men died of the pox a little less, and a little slower.

It was a matter of indifference to me whether the paddle-wheeler delivered its cargo of pox or not. I had been scratched with Jenner's vaccine years ago, and was immune. But most of the gentlemen in my establishment would undoubtedly expire, and I would lose trade.

I am Eleanore Dumont, and I run a house of notorious repute on Front Street, facing the Missouri River, in Fort Benton, Montana Territory. I am amazed at what comes up the river from distant

Independence or even St. Louis. Barrels and crates of all sorts, dandies, preachers, and the pox. Men of all sorts, rarely women, which is why I prosper. Most of the men are gold-fevered.

I am known by another name, Madame Mustache, and I do not discourage it. I am a fat slattern, and I do not discourage them from thinking that, either. I have a coarse dark mustache above my lips. I could easily shave it off, but I don't, because it draws customers, who sit at my table and glance furtively at my hairy lip, a great oddity in a woman, even a slattern, and so they gamble and think about my facial hair, and lose, and I am the better off for it.

Once, an infinity ago, I was beautiful. But that was back in the days of the California Gold Rush, when my gambler husband and I, newly arrived from France, opened an elegant casino. I dealt. The woman-starved miners flocked to my game. I wore decorous clothing, nothing provocative, and I required them to mind their manners. A coarse word earned my rebuke, and ungentlemanly conduct resulted in banishment from my table. They learned swiftly, and those who lost in genteel fashion were allowed to stay until their dust was gone.

I had a little hair above my lip even then, but it was downy and blond and no one noticed, or iaf they did, they did not consider it bizarre. Age and hard living coarsened it, and me. But that is a long story, not important here. *Mon Dieu!* Suffice it to say that I lost my first husband by perforation, and the second tried to squeeze me out of my own business before he died, also of a lead pill, and then I refrained from welcoming men to my bed, and made my living entirely by my own devices.

Now I am simply Madame Mustache, the notorious female entrepreneur of a dozen frontier boom towns where the pickings are easy. Fort Benton fit the bill especially well, because those who arrive here after an easy trip up the Missouri River are ripe for plucking. St. Louis is a long ways away, but they travel in ease. It is my intent always to make sure they are properly motivated by poverty when they leave Fort Benton for the gold fields in Bannack and Virginia City and Last Chance Gulch.

Cards are my vocation. Spirits and the nymphs du prairie are my sidelines. My board and batten business house, facing the turbid river across Front Street in what is considered the rowdiest block in the West, consists of a gambling hall and saloon on the first floor, and a brothel on the second. I will make money by whatever species of sin I can offer, and if there is one *sou* left in the pockets of my customers, I would regard myself a failure.

I recently saw an account of myself published by someone who had wandered through those double doors on Front Street. I was rather taken by it. *She was fat,* he wrote, *showing unmistakably the signs of age. Rouge and powder, apparently applied only half-heartedly, failed to hide the sagging lines of her face, the pouches under her eyes, the general marks of dissipation. Her one badge of respectability was a black silk dress, worn high around her neck."*

I keep the clipping on my dresser. Only the last sentence disappoints me. If the journalist thinks I possess any badge of respectability, he has not looked closely.

Respectable men ignore me. The merchants pretend I don't exist. I rarely see any of them in my establishment, except one or two who sneak up the dark stair. I like it that way.

I was dealing *vingt et un* one early June evening, and losing for a change, the chips sliding from my fingers to the growing heaps of the players semi-circled around me. That's when the news arrived: an anguished whisper that whirled like a dust devil at the bar, and roared like a tornado through my house of pleasure.

"Pox!"

My customers looked nervously about. One pushed outside, leaving the double doors swinging, to examine the river for the sight of that fateful boat. He would look, of course, for the smoke rising over the distant trees that hid the river bend, beyond the island that parted the channels just east of town. But he saw nothing.

I heard the whispers.

"Pox on the *Dance*. Half a dozen passengers at death's door, more feeling poorly, three buried at a riverbank somewheres. Captain's gonna unload 'em right into town here, fixing to start a contagion. Pox, pox, pox...."

"You gonna let 'em in here?" a miner asked me. Actually, he had not mined an ounce of dust in his life. He was off one of the two other packets out of Independence and St. Joseph that were hawsered tightly to the levee. His hands were smooth clerk's hands, and his flannels were stiff out of the box.

"*Monsieur*, play ze game," I said. "Or donate your seat to someone who wants to win riches from me."

He laid out two grimy greenbacks, and I exchanged them for my battered blue chips, and he wagered them. *Bien.* They would soon be mine.

"The pox, it makes bad for business," I said. I showed a jack and six. He motioned for a card and busted. I collected his chips without a smile. I don't waste smiles.

"We have to stop that boat," said Zach, one of my regulars, who I regard fondly as a sort of annuity. "I don't relish fetching the pox, and I never been vaccinated neither. I'd just croak, slow and miserable."

"Shoot the first son-of-a-bitch off that boat that sets foot on the levee," said another. "That's what I say."

"Turn her around and get her outta here. I don't want the sickness," proclaimed a wall-eyed drummer at my table.

I frowned. They weren't focusing on the game, and I was losing money. Speed is what earns profits, as any croupier knows.

"*Messieurs*, bets down or give up your seat."

They played, but I could sense that their minds weren't on the game. An odd quiet had stolen through the saloon, and I did not miss the nervous glances.

A bag-eyed, consumptive bartender who lost his tips at my

table each night folded. "I just think I'll load up a mule and go visit the camps," he said. It was empty talk. He couldn't afford one hoof of a mule.

Men nodded.

"My friend, finish up what you started. You still have three dollars to play," I said.

He started to pick up his chips.

"Double or nothing, turn the card," I said, wanting those dollars.

He shrugged, cut a seven of diamonds, and I cut a jack. I wiped his coin off the table. He looked angry.

The place was stirring. Men slipped through the double doors into the late afternoon sunlight. I was losing trade.

"When is she due?" someone asked.

"Two hours. She's eight or nine miles out."

The gents quit playing. I glared at them, but no one was betting. They were thinking about larger things.

"Maybe I'm gettin' out of here," said one.

"Got no place to go," said another. "I can't even buy a stage ticket."

"We got to stop that damned boat. If I had a cannon, I'd blow it to hell."

"Those packets are well armed," said another.

The other games died too. The chuck-a-luck stopped rattling. The roulette wheel stood idle. Blue haze rose from the poker tables, where men sat with their cards glued to their bellies, thinking about death. The bar was quiet. Men stared through the grimy window at the river front, which was heaped with barrels and crates. And would soon receive a cargo of death.

No disease was more contagious or brutal: high fever, vomiting, headache, delirium, convulsions, diarrhea, and then the eruptions: pink or red spots on the face and hands, and then everywhere, turning into suppurating sores, and if one survived all that, one faced wild itching during the healing. But most died of hemorrhages long before that. The disease lived in clothing, in the very air, and pounced on its victims.

Sacre Bleu! I listened. There wasn't much else to do. I couldn't keep the game going, not with these peckerheads wetting their pants. I couldn't even get one to give up a seat. My house had shut down without my permission, except maybe the girls upstairs. Clap, syphilis, pox, what difference did it make to them?

My customers were nervous.

"I'll find the federal marshal, Wilbert, he's on duty," said one. "All he has to do is tell 'em they can't land...public health, quarantine, all that."

"The marshal? Don't count on him. He's a political paperpusher."

"We could all just line up along that levee with our pieces and tell that captain to shove off."

"Yeah, you think he's gonna bother with that? He's just gonna start unloading."

"You want to stop a sick man getting off?"

"I'd stop him. Shoot him in his tracks."

"Big talk."

"What if they're sick women?"

"Don't let 'em off."

It was all jabber and huff and puff. Outside, I saw a crowd gathering along the levee. They seemed quiet enough, but I knew when that boat hove into view, they'd scatter like field mice. They'd rather face a thousand wild Indians than the pox. They were thinking about the sickness, no doctors in the camp, no hospitals, no medicine, everyone fevered up, lying in some alley with fouled pants, the bodies dumped in the river every day, feeding fish, floating down to St. Louis, half the place sick or dying, pustules on their bodies, puke, thirst, terror.

I was thinking my business was going to hell. I might have to shutter it. Maybe move to Kansas, which is like moving to hell.

"It's just a rumor," I said.

"The hell it's a rumor. Jake Gibbon himself told me...he come busting into town from Cow Island. The *Dance* stopped there to unload some milling stuff for teamsters, and he got wind of it and come racing over here, breaking down two horses."

"Find him," I said. "I want to hear it myself."

"He's spreading the word. Over in The Exchange, and The Elite Saloon, last I knew. Like he's Paul Revere, the redcoats are coming."

I had never heard of Paul Revere. "Drinks on the house," I said. That was my ace in the hole.

Usually that started a stampede for the bar rail, but no one moved. I couldn't believe it. *No one moved.* I folded my cards.

"This game's over. Clear off ze table or I'll keep what's on it," I said.

I watched the cash vanish into purses and pockets.

"The hand of God. He is sending us the plague for our iniquities," said the preacher, looking opium-eyed.

I never learned his name. He really was a preacher, but the drinkingest one I ever saw. Each afternoon for that past month he had showed up, downed a half dozen popskull whiskeys, wiped the sweat off his florid face, eyed the heavenly host, dusted his black suit, and teetered out to save the world. Some said he couldn't keep a congregation back east. He sure lacked one in Fort Benton.

Now he was spreading the fear of perdition around my house of ill repute.

"Get you out!" I snarled. I am usually more civil.

"The hand of God will strike Fort Benton and scythe down its wicked denizens. Just as Sodom and Gomorrah fell, so will Fort Benton."

They were all listening.

"It's just a rumor," I said. But they were all staring into their opened graves and I might as well be talking to the dead.

That's how it went. No one had a plan. The mob collected along the muddy levee, waiting for its own doom in the dying sun, which gilded the yellow bluffs across the river. My sporting house was all but deserted.

Then, faintly, something changed.

"Here she comes!" someone yelled.

I couldn't see anything, but then, I can hardly see the pasteboards these days with my cataracts. Sure enough, first there was a disturbance of the air downriver, a flight of crows, faint smoke, and then the rattle of the escapement, the staccato thunder that announced the imminent arrival of a packet from below, from what they called the States out here, because Fort Benton just wasn't in the States.

The death ship rounded the bend, its smoke disturbing the sky, white plumes of steam ricocheting against the cobalt eastern horizon. The horizontal sun gilded its white enamel and made it glow like a grinning skull. It slowed; the river is tricky here. It whistled its arrival, shattering the silence. A stir ran through the mob, and the entire crowd backed up ten or twenty steps, smitten by an unseen and murderous hand.

I peered through my window. Business was lousy and going to get worse. I stared at the emptied-out saloon, with my consumptive dealers slouched over their tables and filling the spittoons, and the bar men standing like aproned statues.

Only the preacher remained, grinning wolfishly, as if he had personally called down the plague.

"I haven't made a dollar in fifteen minutes," I snapped.

My nymphs du prairie emerged from the stairwell in their wrappers, weeping copiously. Lulu was a little tetched, which is how I acquired her, but even Maybelle was whining.

"You are not permitted down here," I snapped.

"Are we going to die?" Maybelle asked.

"Any time," I replied. "From clap or consumption or opium or cyanide. It will be no loss."

They shrank back.

I peered out the window. The glistening white riverboat was drifting into the levee now. Passengers and crew lined the rail, waiting to debark.

"Isn't there a man in town?" I asked.

No one replied.

"Well, then it's up to a woman," I said.

Hanging from pegs along one wall were assorted weapons on their belts. I required that they be placed there upon entering. Gambling, drinking, and whoring stirred up the heat in men, and I didn't want any more blood on my plank floors than necessary. It was bad for business.

I eyed the row of revolvers, and selected a slick black gun belt with a pair of clean, newly blued Navy revolvers poking from their nests.

I plucked it and wrapped it around my bulging middle, black belt over black silk, and hitched the belt tight, feeling the weight of those six-guns.

Then I plunged through the double doors into the twilit gloom of Front Street, and shouldered my way through a pack of gutless sopranos until I stood on the levee, scarcely twenty feet from the closing packet.

The captain, dressed in natty blue, with a visored cap over his bewhiskered face, peered down at me from the hurricane deck, in front of the pilot house. Good. His river men were readying the gangway. Passengers with baggage in hand stood ready.

The boat slid silently to shore, but no one reached for the hawsers that the boatmen threw.

I pulled those twin engines of death from their sheaths and pointed both of them directly at the captain.

"No one gets off this boat!" I yelled hoarsely.

That caught the attention of the crowd.

"Madam," the captain replied through a megaphone, "put down those revolvers and you won't get hurt."

"You got pox on board?"

He nodded, reluctantly.

"Then put on the steam and get out. No one with the pox lands here."

"Madam, I have not come two thousand miles just to turn around with my cargo. I have one hundred ninety-eight tons to unload."

"You heard me. If that gangway touches land, you'll be the first to die. Anyone steps on that gangway, he's dead."

I saw now that several of the passengers were armed, some with rifles and some with their own revolvers, but the captain wasn't, and I kept my revolvers pointing straight at him.

"You risk your life, madam."

"No, I'm risking yours. You heard me. You turn this bateau around and go away."

"And what am I to do with this cargo?"

"Take it somewhere else. And take the pox with you."

By now the crowd behind me was stirring. Those closest to me were sliding out of danger from flying lead. It wasn't but a moment and I was entirely alone, a fat woman on the levee, with all those bravos and knights of Fort Benton sulking in shadow out of harm's way.

The captain stirred.

The boat bumped land, and began sliding along the levee, drawn by the current. It would collide with the *Waverly* just downstream.

The captain turned to the helmsman and tugged on bells. A great chuff of steam erupted from the escapement, and the *Walter B. Dance* shuddered to life. Its wheel turned over thunderously, and with a mighty splash halted the drifting vessel just twenty yards from the *Waverly*, and soon the pox boat gained against the current and pulled away. There was precious little turning room in that channel, but the skilled helmsman swung the boat around, and the packet slowly thrashed eastward and vanished into the twilight, leaving a strange hush in its wake.

Only then did I lower my revolvers.

"You did it!" someone cried. "Madame Mustache did it!"

"You spared us the pox!"

"You chased him off!"

"Madam, you have spared the entire city of Fort Benton."

"Lot of help I got from you brave gents," I said, stuffing my borrowed revolvers back in their sheaths. My arms were tired.

"Hurrah for Madame Mustache!"

They were clapping me on the back, a rude American indignity I never would have permitted earlier in my life. They were cheering, tossing hats, whistling, discharging their pieces with ear-splitting volleys, laughing, bawling like cattle, strutting as if they had faced down the devil, grinning, and building up a grand thirst.

I survived the cosseting, entered my notorious house, and unbuckled the borrowed gun belt. I never did find out whose it was. But his revolvers had rescued the city.

"Drinks on the house," I said, hoping it would not be too costly a gesture. But one drink would lead to another, and I stood to make a tidy profit this day.

They crowded in, all these smelly, rank, unshaven men, filled my bawdy house with their good humor.

"We should erect a statue to you, madam." That from one of the town's leading citizens, a merchant who had never deigned to speak to me before.

"You pay for any erection in here," I said, trying to get to my table. But they would not let me. My barkeeps were pouring red-eye and popskull by the gallon. I never gave away good whiskey, and the mob was downing the stuff with single gulps.

"Madam, you have saved the day," said the preacher. "You are the horn of our salvation. You have driven away the plague. Out of the tenderness of your womanly heart, you have poured compassion upon the vulnerable and the frightened."

I laughed. I haven't laughed in years.

Compassion," I said, and wheezed cheerfully at that preposterous idea. "Compassion you call it? Ha! You are an idiot. Tonight I will claw more gold out of everyone than I do in a month. Here now, let me get to my table so you can donate your greenbacks to me. It was a purely commercial proposition."

THE GREAT FILIBUSTER
OF 1975

Now, I know you're going to disapprove. You'll be shaking your head, frowning, and concluding that I am the ugly American; that I threatened the comity of nations, acted recklessly, was utterly insensitive to the world's poor, and am stupid besides. And that's just for starters.

Actually, I would agree with you. I was all of the above, and I am quite contrite. Or at least ninety percent of me is contrite. The other ten percent — well, you have to understand that I am an aging juvenile delinquent. I look back upon that awful deed not as a moment of shame or folly, but as my own glorious footnote to History. After all, do you know of anyone else — even one soul — who has added to the territory of the United States? Especially by stealing it from a neighbor? Ah, now I have your attention! I committed a *filibuster* against Mexico.

But I have gotten ahead of myself. In 1975 I was at loose ends, having been put out of work by the great oil crisis and recession. It was a bad time for the United States. The sheiks had turned off the spigot. There was the little matter of Watergate. A lot of us were out of work, including me, John Arnold, indirectly descended from Benedict Arnold but the family doesn't make it known.

By trade I am a newspaper editor. But in 1975 I had no trade at all, having been released from the desperate grasp of a certain Midwestern metropolitan daily that I will not mention for fear of embarrassing its stockholders. I am also a veteran bachelor, having attended a wife briefly in my youth and finding the whole arrangement without merit. I prefer to spend my entire salary on myself. At least when I have a salary, which I didn't in 1975.

As long as I was at loose ends, and the chances of getting a job in a recession were nil, I thought I'd squander my savings on adventure. So I traded my Midwestern Buick for a used pickup truck and headed West, intending to end up in whatever trouble I could get into, wherever the wind blew me. That proved to be the Rancho Oro Blanco, right smack on the Mexican border of Arizona, southwest of Tucson, a place just about as remote as one can get.

Oro Blanco was, in fact, a venerable guest ranch, but so hidden that only the most intrepid guests ever found it. It spread over the eastern edge of the Altar Valley, a vast mountain-girt desert plain that extended north and south, from deep in Sonora well into Arizona. To reach it, one drove to the weary little town of Arivaca, perched solemnly on an arid plain and existing only because its few inhabitants were too tired and broke to depart, and from there one traversed an endless dirt road that meandered south and west, through cholla-choked cañons, and ocotillo-crowned hills, until suddenly one burst out upon a watered delta dotted with cotton-woods and verdant grasses, all of it shocking green. Here a giant arroyo burst out of the hills and emptied into the valley. It was dry, of course, like everything else in the Sonora Desert, but not far under its rough, sandy bed lay a water table that was the foundation of the Rancho Oro Blanco, the White Gold Ranch.

During the winter months the ranch did a lively trade, offering a thin warmth and horseback riding and bird-watching to guests from all over the world. The Oro Blanco was a venerable place, over two hundred years old, and owed its existence to a Spanish land grant dating back to the 1750s. The ancient dried-mud buildings hadn't changed much. The adobe guest quarters had beehive fire-places and ocotillo ramadas. The corrals had been built of mesquite and rawhide. The old *rancho* itself had terra cotta tile floors, *vigas*, thick adobe walls strong enough to fend off the Apaches, and an array of heavy Mexican colonial furniture.

I had arrived in May, when the temperatures were already topping a hundred each afternoon, and not a guest was in sight. A room might be had for very little during the Sonoran summer, and the use of the big kitchen came with it. The *rancho* did not employ much help during those furnace months. There was only the manager and his wife, and one wrangler to look after the dude string, as the saddle horses were called. Assorted Mexicans drifted in and out, on mysterious errands, occasionally as day labor. Whether they were legally on the north side of the line I could not say.

I settled in. The place enchanted me. There I was, in the middle of nowhere, three hours from Tucson but it may as well have been three weeks. They let me fool with a gentle horse, and if I got up at six I could get in a good ride before it got hot. The place twittered with desert birds of such plumage and color as I had never seen, as if I had entered a land of a thousand fluorescent parrots.

I didn't know what to do with myself, but what did it matter?

The border itself was nothing but an ordinary four-strand barbed wire fence stretching arrow-straight in a southeast-northwest direction there. The desert on the other side was more ravaged by grazing than land on the United States side, but just as unpopu-lated and mysterious. The fence, I learned, was private property; it belonged to the *rancho*, not the government. And its upkeep was not shared by the Mexican ranchers on the other side, who were too poor to maintain it. The border was demarcated by small white obelisks at five-mile intervals. One stood on the *rancho*. Occasional wire ranch gates had been built into the border fence here and there, and I could only surmise what for. Sometimes I saw footprints in the sand at those gates. There was traffic I knew nothing about, that probably passed in the night.

During my forays into the kitchen I got to know my hosts, Cap and Marcy Granville, and the wrangler, a blond kid from Wyoming named Willie something or other. If the Granvilles had social graces they reserved them for the guests in season. During the hot, dry summer days of doing almost nothing, they grumbled at each other, complained, and vanished into their rooms for endless *siestas*. Willie was more taciturn, and apart from working some green-broke horses in the cool dawn, forking some alfalfa hay, checking the wells, and smoking some contraband under his ocotillo arbor at twilight, he mostly slept. He obviously intended to squander the fierce Sonora summer letting his thin blond beard grow to perfect scruffiness while avoiding declarations longer than three words. That suited me fine. I was more interested in the lizards and Gila monsters and exotic pink desert rattlers than in the riff-raff.

In spite of their best efforts not to be sociable, I got to know them well. The summer isolation does that. Just when you think you've left the whole world behind, you hanker for companionship. I was quite content to spend days and hours saying nothing, avoiding the others, and doing nothing. After twenty years of laboring in the vineyards, I wanted to do nothing at all. The exotic land, so harsh and handsome, was enough for my soul at that time.

But society intrudes, even in that silent, remote corner of the nation. And where else but the kitchen? They cooked their meals, just as I cooked mine, and soon enough we were eating together.

Captain (where the title came from I don't know; there was nothing military about him, thank God) Theophilius Granville, it turned out, was a burly carrot-haired natural boor as well as the world's greatest expert, but he had the saving grace of conceit. He thought little of the neighbors to the south, who he called "our brown brothers". I thought at first he was a home-grown racist, but he wasn't, exactly. Chauvinist would be a better word. He was simply jaundiced and cynical.

If the brown brothers had let a diesel engine burn up for lack of crankcase oil, that was something to nod knowingly about. If the brown brothers drilled a well in the bottom of an arroyo that drew off village sewage and they all got sick, that was something for Cap to dwell upon with sheer joy. If the brown mothers spent all their loose *pesos* on expensive Pampers at the port of Sasabe instead of changing diapers, that was something delicious to rail about. Cap found evidence every day to fortify his views. I found his bilious observations infectious in spite of myself. They were an entertainment that continued nonstop to while away a hot empty summer. The more time he spent with me, the less guarded he became, and after a few weeks I came to know Cap Granville as a rural raptor whose own vulpine esteem fed on the carcasses of his neighbors across the line.

Mexico offended him enormously, hugely, like some giant trash heap in the middle of Newport Beach. And there it was, just beyond the four-strand barbed-wire fence, this monster of Granville's indignation, this habitat of cretins who guzzled *cerveza* that tasted like varnish, slaved in an adobe brick factory for eight cents an hour, and knifed each other on weekends and holy days for sport.

Marcy was kinder. She was Earth Woman, embracing brown brothers and sisters to her generous bosom. But I preferred to listen to the refreshing and uncivilized bile issuing from the Captain, which was an improvement over the bland talk radio one could sometimes pick up. Cap was an original, and from his jaundiced soul I fashioned a good idea of life across the border, a life I never witnessed because across that mysterious fence was nothing but barren rock, ocotillo, cholla, and silence.

Neighboring the ranch to the west was the small, crowded yard of a refrigerator smuggler, who dwelled on a hectare or so carved out of the great *hacienda* some eons ago, some peon's reward for a life of servitude. His *casa* could be reached only by traversing a violent two-rut road that wound and teetered westward into the broad Altar Valley and eventually joined a larger ranch road, and finally the unpaved Arizona highway to Sasabe. The refrigerator smuggler, one ChiChi Juarez, made his living by running used appliances into Mexico in his battered Nineteen-Fifties vintage-gray Ford stock truck. His adobe house stood so close to the line that he could spit into Mexico from his window. But his weedy clay yard was a phenomenon. Everywhere I looked, I beheld cancerous Maytags and Frigidaires, rusty swamp coolers, venerable Whirlpools and Kenmores and *Generalissimo* Electrics, all of them the offscouring of prosperous Tucson. You would suppose he was running an outdoor laundromat. No nearby wire gate in the border fence ever revealed tire tracks through it, but every few weeks this amazing collection of rusty white rectangles would vanish, and then ChiChi's clay yard would be the home only of *ninos* and tarantulas and Gila monsters, along with old batteries, mufflers, washing machine innards, and carburetors.

The source of ChiChi's wealth was simple. Mexico imposed a stiff import duty on manufactured goods, a duty equal to the cost of the appliance, and the result was that Mexico's *campesinos* could not afford new or even used washers or refrigerators or stoves or dryers or air conditioners or coffee makers or freezers. So it became ChiChi's inspired vocation to relieve suffering south of the border, by purchasing these objects in Tucson and then periodically running down dusty Sonoran trails, far from the eyes of the *Federales*, or maybe right under their eyes if he filled their extended palms, and sold his rusty iron in Hermosillo.

I considered ChiChi a hero, making Arizona a cleaner state and relieving the poor of their suffering. He could barely speak English so I had little commerce with him, but he smiled a great deal, displaying a fine gold incisor. And judging from the perpetual distended condition of his *esposa*, I knew that his greatest achievement on earth was manufacturing *ninos*, which he produced as reliably as stoves and washing machines.

And so my Sonoran summer progressed. The heat deepened. As May cooked into June, the furnace heat stifled the impulse to do anything but lie abed and enjoy the dry breezes wafting through open windows. Even the exotic birds headed for cover midday. I had never experienced a heat so oppressive or pervasive or inescapable, for there was no air conditioning at Rancho Oro Blanco except for a swamp cooler in the Granvilles' adobe. But I rejoiced. For the first time in my forty-two years, I was doing absolutely nothing, and not all the promptings of conscience warning me against a squandered and ruined life persuaded me to do anything other than wander about like some war-ruined veteran, which in a commercial way, I was. I was adrift among sun-blasted rock heaps, cactus, scaly creatures, scorpions, and gaudy birds.

The Granvilles warned me that the summer monsoon season would start late in June, around San Juan's Feast Day. These would be sharp showers and would be over fast, and sometimes the rain would not even reach the superheated desert floor.

The day began just the same as any other, burning bright with a brassy sky and a ferocious sun. But then, to my surprise, clouds built over the mountains, and formed into towers of cumulus, sometimes tens of thousands of feet high, so one peered upward into a world of white walls. It did not rain that day, but plainly something had changed. The air was somehow different, softer, gentler, like baby's flesh. The following day the towers of cloud increased, and some of them formed black bottoms and I saw slanting streaks of gray rain falling from them. Lightning flickered in the heart of these white soldiers of the sky, and sometimes I heard the distant rumble of thunder. But I had not yet witnessed more than a dozen drops of rain falling on the parched Sonoran Desert, and I suspected the whole show might be smoke and mirrors. But I did enjoy the sudden freshets, the cold downdrafts, the whirlwinds of damp air that eddied across the *rancho*. And down in Mexico it was plainly raining, great gray sheets obscuring the horizon.

The third day of the monsoon season began sullenly, with angry clouds obscuring the heavens. These had flat purple bottoms, and rose so high I could scarcely spot the bold blue of the sky. Midmorning the wind kicked up, whirling dust, rattling desert sand against dusty windows, chattering doors, bending the palo verde and willow trees, and shooting icy tendrils into my room. I stared anxiously upon a grim heaven, bruised purple and black, that had driven Arizona's blue sky out of sight.

The rain arrived like cannon shot, rattling off the tile and tin roofs, banging the earth, raising puffs of dust, thumping against window glass, leaving muddy streaks as it coursed downward. A hum built slowly, an eerie whispering rumble unlike anything I had ever heard, and then sheets of rain swept in, opaque curtains of rain blasting everything in their path, instantly turning the barren yellow clay into brown gumbo. I felt the whole earth vibrate with the deluge; the rain gusted under the broad eaves intended to protect the adobe from water; it sluiced over the ground, instantly flooding every hollow, cutting channels before my eyes. And in the midst of this roar of water, came lightning so constant it resembled the flickering of an arc light, and drum rolls of thunder that shot atmospheric bullets that I feared would collapse the building or rip away its sheet metal roof.

This Sonora storm did not abate in minutes. Noon passed without change, and the afternoon turned black. Through the watery windows I beheld a lake; there seemed to be no dry ground anywhere. Instant rivers formed, scouring the corrals of the horse muck in them, knocking plants flat, pushing in around my front door and onto my tile floor, pooling at the base of my beehive fireplace. The electricity quit, and I could do naught but gaze upon a fearsome gray world in which visibility ceased scarcely ten paces distant. Rarely could I see the other guest quarters, or the main buildings of the *rancho*.

What pierced my consciousness then was a new sort of roar, the sound of rolling water tumbling ever downslope. I knew the great arroyo was running. It was called El Coronel, the Colonel, the wash that collected all the waters from the naked mountains to the east and north, and flumed them into Mexico. It was El Coronel that gave the *rancho* its wells, which supplied its water table, which nurtured the cottonwoods and willows and palo verdes and a hundred other desert shrubs and trees, which made the *rancho* an island of bright green even in the season of sun-baked drought.

El Coronel was roaring, and I ached to know whether it would wash away my building, or other ranch buildings. By two the storm had abated, and occasional shafts of sun poked through the gray cloud banks. But El Coronel still roared, carrying hundreds of millions of gallons of water with it, straight through the *rancho* and across the border, where the arroyo flattened and widened into a great *playa* visible from the border fence.

That's when I heard Cap shouting.

"Hey, Arnold, we need you!"

I could not imagine why, but hesitantly stepped outside into the mild drizzle, which wetted my jeans and tee shirt. The light rain was not unpleasant.

I found Cap, Marcy, and Willie all awaiting my presence, water dripping off them.

"Border fence is down," Cap explained. "Washout. This was a fifty-year storm, and El Coronel took two, three hundred yards of fence with it."

We slogged over surprisingly firm clay to the border, a quarter mile south, and beheld the devastation. The tan water still churned through the broad arroyo. The fence was nowhere in sight. I could not even see where the break started and ended.

"Jaysas," said Willie. That was about as exclamatory as he ever got.

Cap squinted at me. "We gotta rebuild fast. Keep the horses in. If they get into Mexico, we'll never see 'em again."

"I thought you told me the Mex ranchers always returned stock."

"Well, yeah, but these are good horses, and if the brown brothers find them, we ain't gonna see them again."

"Well, couldn't Willie get them into the pens?"

"Scattered to hell and gone now. Could be miles from here, up on higher ground." He fixed me with his pale gaze. "We gonna build fence. Fast. No one eats around here until we get that fence up."

I had never built barbed-wire fence in my life.

"Yeah, I'll help," I said. "But don't count on me knowing what I'm doing."

"Willie and me, we'll show you. Everyone here works, including Marcy."

I eyed that brown river dubiously. "How deep is that?"

"We'll find out."

Over the next hour we collected spools of barbed wire, staples, clips, a wire-stretcher, which worked in some manner beyond my fathoming, sledge-hammers, a dozen metal posts, a few twisted mesquite posts, spades, hammers, and other mysterious gear, and loaded it into the battered ranch pickup, all the while keeping a wary eye on the border for renegade horses or Mexican *bandidos* creeping up to snatch the entire herd of the hated *gringos*.

We piled into the ancient International Harvester and Cap steered it toward the arroyo, spraying muddy water over the windshield. By the time we returned to the border, El Coronel had reduced itself to a braided trickle. The unfenced border yawned at us. The last of the storm clouds vanished, and the late afternoon sun shot golden light over the drenched Sonoran Desert. The quiet was eerie. The cool air was intoxicating. On the Mexican side, a vast silvery lake, a *playa*, shimmered where only tawny clay had stretched before. We began looking for the border fence, which was nowhere in sight.

I walked into Mexico, oddly enjoying the undocumented visit. Not a soul observed our progress. We found the west wires first, twisted and tangled on the ground, the metal posts lying flat but still connected to the barbed wire. We followed that for some distance until we came to undamaged fence.

"At least it's mostly still here," Cap said. "But we're going to have to free every post from the wire and start over."

The downed wire at the eastern end was shorter because the ground rose above the arroyo.

"All right, Willie and Marcy, you work at this end, free up those posts, and John and I will work the west end," Cap said. "We gotta hurry...get this done before dark, or at least a couple strands anyway. Wear gloves."

That was good advice. It wasn't long before my hands were bleeding, even with gloves on.

The wire was fastened to the steel posts with little clips which were the devil's own invention. But slowly we freed post after post and left them lying in the sodden ground, well inside Mexico. Off in the distance, we could see Willie and Marcy slowly working toward us, and sometimes even hear the murmur of their conversation.

"Damned Messicans. Why don't they help us? They get the benefit of the fence without donating a dime," Cap grumbled, wiping a bloody hand on his jeans. "They just feast on us. You know that over in Sasabe, half the women live on Pima County welfare checks? They get a little domestic work up to Tucson, and next thing you know, they get unemployment comp and stuff like that, and that keeps 'em flush for a year and then they work a little on a green card and go back to sucking money out of the country," he muttered. "If they didn't have suckers like us paying their way, they'd earn fifty dollars a year in the adobe brick factory."

I could see the direction his thoughts were rolling and kept quiet. The work was exhausting, wet, and miserable. At least it wasn't cold. The temperature had cooled down into the eighties and the air was pleasant.

El Coronel had swept the ranch fence forty or fifty yards into

Mexico. We worked steadily, freeing the posts and wires, until finally we reached the broken ends of our strands. Marcy and Willie had finished before us, and were hauling posts back toward the border.

"I don't know how we'll ever get the damned fence straight," Cap grumbled. "We don't have the equipment to lay it right along the line. We'd need a surveyor...."

We rested a while, sucked Coronas around the back end of the pickup. The air had cleared and now we could see up and down the international border. We could even see the white pylon far to the east, but not the one to the west. I can date the filibuster to that very moment.

"To hell with all that," Cap said. "We gotta keep the brown brothers from borrowing our horses."

"We could eyeball it," I said. "I'll go to the first upright post to the west, and Marcy can go to the first standing post to the east, and we can sight down a line and drive a few in as sort of guidelines. We'll yell the directions to you."

Cap snorted. "They're always getting welfare checks from us," he said, a remark I did not yet fathom.

Willie got the idea before I did, and grinned crookedly from pot-shot eyes.

"We're just gonna bend this here fence a little," Cap said.

I thought he was joking, but he dropped a steel fence post slightly inside Mexico, walked about a rod, and set down another one a couple of feet farther south. "Pound these in," he said. "Get that little flange part of the post well into the clay. It's soft."

He began laying out the posts in a great arc that bent gently southward. Willie began hammering the posts at the east end, and I pounded on the westerly ones, while Marcy sorted the tangled strands of wire as best she could. Some of it would have to be cut out and thrown away.

Cap returned to help me.

"We'll get into trouble," I said. "They'll just make us do it right."

"When were you gelded, Arnold?"

"I don't think this is a good idea."

"It's called getting even."

"For what?"

"What are you, some wimp?"

That hurt. Well, the hell with it. I figured I'd be leaving soon anyway. My money would run out. Maybe the recession would be over. I'd get away from that crazy place.

Hammering posts drained me of whatever strength I had left. The rain-softened clay accepted the steel readily enough, but there were a lot of steel posts to pound home, and a lot of rock in the way, and I knew I would never become a ranch hand if I could help it.

The air continued to clear and as the sun settled lower, it lit the land with a golden light that gilded the arrow-straight border fence. We were clearly building fence five or six yards into Mexico. I kept eyeing the mesquite trees south of the line, waiting for a squad of *Federales* to pounce, but we saw nothing, not even a stray cow.

I kept worrying and wimping. The rest built fence and laughed and celebrated the liberation of turf from the Republic of Mexico. I have to give them credit. Once they got into the mood of it, they were transformed into a gang of filibusters scything through prostrate Mexico like a small army.

We got the posts in around six, and took a break, but Cap wanted the wire up before dark, so we started in again. The wire-stretcher proved to be useless. We needed to anchor it to a good wooden post in order to ratchet the wire taut, and there were no good wooden posts, nor was our new fence a straight line. So we tugged, bloodied our hands, wrapped pieces of barbed wire around the metal posts, and jerry-built a border fence. Now, with the sun low, we could clearly see the bulge. I guessed we were copping maybe an eighth of an acre, and being very bad neighbors, but I had shut up and was working silently. Willie and Cap were sucking beer now, tossing the empties into the truck bed, pissing on the posts, and making smart remarks about Mexican fence-builders.

Cap justified it all. "If it'd been them, instead of us, they'd have snatched twice as much ground," he said, and belched.

We got the top and bottom strands stretched, after a fashion. That would be enough to keep stray livestock in, and we were pretty beat.

Cap squinted at the dying sun. "That'll hold until tomorrow," he said. "But, Willie, you go find them horses and run 'em into the pens if you can."

Willie nodded. We threw the loose gear into the old truck and rattled back to the *rancho*, feeling we had done a lick of work. The ranch looked strange, scoured clean of every plant and stick and pebble. The lower three feet of the adobe buildings were stained brown in spite of the broad eaves intended to keep rain away from the mud walls.

"That 'dobe plaster, it's got some emulsion in it that resists water," Cap said. "They sell it up at Tucson. Got put to the test this time, but I don't see any crumbling mud heaps."

The Rancho Oro Blanco would be all right, but I wasn't sure the border would be. Someday, some federal official accompanied by some Mexican, would come knocking.

I slept hard that night.

The next day, a breezy and balmy one, we finished the fence. We packed our tools and hiked to the east edge of the arroyo. From the rising slope there, one could peer across the bottoms of the El Coronel, and discover that certain territory bordering Arizona, formerly in the possession of the Republic of Mexico, had been transferred to the Stars and Stripes.

"Ain't that purty?" Cap asked. "Serves them brown brothers right."

I just shook my head, wimpishly, but Cap was watching.

"We've made history. We should go down in the books," he said.

The rest of the Sonoran summer passed quietly, and eventually

I left the desert and found a job in an Illinois town surrounded by endless cornfields. It was such a bucolic place that I began to regale the locals with yarns about my Sonoran adventures. Especially my filibuster. Like all good stories, this one grew with the telling. The good burghers, for whom I produced a five-days-a-week paper, listened to my border tales with secret envy and vast disapproval, and the more they disapproved, the grander my filibuster became. No longer did I assert that we had commandeered an eighth of an acre. The figure grew to half, then one, and finally "several". No longer was I, John Arnold, the wimp of the filibuster expedition, worried about unneighborly conduct and international incidents. Instead I became the swashbuckler, a filibuster armed to the teeth with Howitzers at my hips, an inciter of uproars, and a famous liar.

I relished my notoriety. Who else, after all, had increased the territory of the United States? I don't know whether the fence ever got fixed or rebuilt along the line. My guess is that it still bulges south, and the local ranchers on either side still return the strays without telling the officials about it. That's the way life is in Sonora. I never saw Cap and Marcy and Willie again; they are merely phantasms now. But together, we were a conquering army.

THE TINHORN'S LADY

Now, I know you're going to disapprove. You'll be shaking your head, frowning. The jangle of the cowbell at the door of his Cedar Street cottage awakened Sandor Gollancz from a desolate dream. He had arranged the cowbell because he was a heavy sleeper. Sometimes people needed a doctor fast. He sighed, stabbed his toes into slippers, scratched a Lucifer, and lit his bedside lamp, and lighted his way to the front door.

There he beheld a man he knew, Billy Behind the Ace, a swaggering tinhorn from the sporting district. Austin didn't lack for tinhorns or sports to mine the miners. This one, a swarthy skeletal fellow with a left facial tic and black hair parted down the middle, operated a faro layout in the back of the Mammoth Saloon. His abrasiveness had become legendary, and he could out-brag the entire Sazerac Liars Club.

"Get your duds on and help Rosa," he said, peremptorily.

Gollancz yawned. "I was just dreaming of a woman like her," he said. "What time is it?"

"Three. Hurry."

"What seems to be the trouble?"

"The ague."

"Tell me exactly."

"Chills so bad her body shook all morning. Then a hot, dry fever. Then she started to sweat. She's delirious."

"Why didn't you send for me earlier?"

"I was attending to my business."

"Vivax malaria, I think," Gollancz said. "All right. Give me a minute."

"You'll damned well hurry. If she dies, so will you."

Gollancz ignored the ruffian and retreated with the lamp to his bedroom. He pulled up black trousers over his nightshirt, stuffed his stockingless toes into high-top shoes, laced up, and hurried to his office where he kept his Gladstone at the ready. There would be sulphate of quinine in it. Rosa would require at least ten grains every eight hours.

They plunged into a hushed, starry night. The soft desert air felt pleasant on the doctor's unshaven face. He could not say why he had come to Austin, Nevada, except for the sheer exuberant adventure of it. Budapest seemed another life altogether: settled, green, mannered, ironic, and brimming with quiet laughter and flirtation. Not a proper place for a restless man such as himself. Now he was on another continent, fluently speaking a second tongue, camped in a vast and arid wasteland, with only the stark Toiyabe Mountains for solace. He scarcely knew what grass looked like any more. Not that it mattered. He had never loved life more madly.

Billy Behind the Ace — what a peculiar *nom de guerre* that was — trotted toward Virginia Street, and into a whitewashed dwelling house behind the saloon. Blackness engulfed them as they made their way blindly up a wooden stair that echoed hollowly. When the sport opened the door, Gollancz blinked away the lamplight from within the parlor, and followed the tinhorn into a bedroom that exuded the subtle scents of fever and desperation.

The tinhorn lit the light on the bed table.

He had seen Rosa in the Mammoth, dealing faro. Every male in

Austin had made that pilgrimage time and time again. Half the male population swore Rosa was the most beautiful woman on earth. She had thrown off the coverlets. Her white cotton nightgown was soaked and translucent, and rode high on her golden thighs. The sheen of sweat lay upon her neck and her upper chest above the scoop of the nightgown. Her exquisite fine-boned face lay in a nest of tangled black hair. He had never seen a woman so galvanizing. Something Hispanic or Creole radiated from her golden flesh, and maybe Indian and black, too — along with desperate fever. She did not open her eyes.

"Quit staring and fix her up."

The tinhorn had it right: Sandor Gollancz had been paralyzed by the sight. He swiftly settled beside her on the creaking bed and put a hand on her wet forehead. Fever leapt up at him. He found a racing, light pulse. The hot, dry stage had passed; she was deep into the sweating stage. The thermometer rose to one hundred and four degrees.

"Rosa," he said sharply.

She moaned incoherently.

"How long has she been sweating like this?" he asked the tinhorn.

"This evening. She had a hot fever all afternoon. Chills this morning. A headache last night."

"When was the last attack?"

"Seven or eight weeks ago."

"How many has she had?"

"I don't know. That's how she was when I won her."

"She'll have more fevers in about two days. Get me a tumbler of water," the doctor said.

While he waited, he extracted a pasteboard box containing ten-grain tablets of the cinchona extract, and pulled out two. He doubted he could get her to swallow the tablets.

"Help me," he said to the tinhorn. "I want her sitting up when I give her the medicine." He would have lifted the woman himself, and probably ended up staring into the bore of the tinhorn's Derringer.

It took several attempts to get the tablet down Rosa. She gagged. She spit out the pill. He poked the second one back on her tongue, feeling fever radiate from her, and washed it down her throat. Then the tinhorn lowered Rosa to the tumbled bed.

"You're lucky. There aren't many fevers I can help," Gollancz said. "If it were the other kind of ague...the African...she probably would die or end up in blackwater fever."

"Don't you leave now."

"I don't intend to. If you'd like to do something useful, dampen a cloth and wipe her down. Cool down her fever."

"You do it."

"I'd prefer that you do it." Rosa fevered him too much. His profession warred with his instincts.

The tinhorn grunted, and handed Gollancz a cool wet towel, which he applied to her forehead, neck, arms, and ankles, sometimes handing it back to the tinhorn for another soaking.

Rosa moaned now and then but didn't come around as Gollancz applied the compresses.

"You told me you won her," the doctor said, surrendering to his curiosity.

"With the cut of a card."

"What was the wager?"

"Everything I owned. My faro layout. My ten-grand faro bank. I had to have her. I cut the deck first and pulled a three of spades. I knew I'd lost. But the sport she was with cut a deuce of clubs. So I won. She was worth it."

"And what if you'd lost?"

The tinhorn shrugged. "Work for someone else. I can deal faro, keep cases, be a look-out. Someday I'd make a new stake."

"How?"

The tinhorn smiled. "This is the West. The chances come all the time."

"Who was she with?" Gollancz phrased the question delicately.

"A riverboat gambler who dressed like a deacon. Emile Roque. But now she's mine."

"Ah, what does Rosa have to say about this?"

"She has no say."

"Was she glad when you won her?"

"She cried."

"Is she happy now?"

"Who cares? It's not your business."

"It may be," said Gollancz. An idea was shaping his diagnosis. Rosa had not come out of her delirium. Far from it. Instead of escaping this febrile episode, she lay locked within it. He fed her a half-tablet of quinine, doing it himself this time as Billy Behind the Ace glowered jealously. She felt limp and hot when he lifted her. He forced her to sip water, but she gagged and he stopped. She was becoming seriously dehydrated.

"Let me be," she murmured, never opening her eyes.

Gollancz sat quietly through the small hours, observing no change. This sort of febrile crisis was uncommon. She had sunk into delirium, and yet delirium was extremely rare in this strain of the disease. She didn't have the African variety, so dangerous and usually fatal. But she had succumbed to this milder, repetitive variety as if it were the falciparum kind. At last he concluded that something larger than the ague affected Rosa. She suffered a profound malady of soul or spirit. Rosa's soul was weighted with despair. The woman was trying to die.

Yes, that was it. She had been reduced to slavery. One heartless gambler had wagered her. Another gambler had bet on her. Neither had cared an iota about her feelings. She had become chattel, a plaything, a fabulous beauty to show off, even a source of income. He knew something about this woman. She often dealt faro, and usually attracted a throng of hungry, admiring miners. So this Billy Behind the Ace was exploiting her, and her heart had broken, and now in her degradation she hoped to escape the cage of life, so her soul might fly free like a canary suddenly loosed.

Ah, these Americans! A new race formed out of many. Admirable, adventuresome — and barbarous! What unthinkable conduct! Gambling for a woman without the slightest attention to her wishes. Ah, how those tinhorns had circled around her. The first one had seduced her and took her away from a respectable life; now this one was oppressing her, and she was trying to die.

The tinhorn had retired to the horsehair sofa in the parlor, and once in a while Gollancz could hear him snore or toss. Just as well. If the man were hovering around, Gollancz would probably vent his fury on the bounder. Instead, he had the bedroom to himself, and he sat quietly in a Morris chair, gazing into the night. He was growing weary. He had been robbed of sleep many times; that was part of his calling. But this night he felt depressed. He turned the wick down and waited in the close, choking dark, listening to her labored breathing and pondering the strangeness of life.

In the gray light of first dawn he sensed a change. He slid to her bedside and discovered a dry, cool forehead under his hand and a serene, steady breath.

"Who are you?" she said.

Startled, he drew back. She was gazing at him. No delirium or confusion in her face this time. "A surgeon. Sandor Gollancz."

"Where are you from?"

"A place near Budapest."

"Is that in Africa?"

"No, my dear, it is part of the Austro-Hungarian empire."

"Wherever that is. Yoah heah to fix my ague?"

He could sort out these strains of Yankee English well enough to know she was from the Confederacy. "We can help it...we can't cure it. I've given you quinine. Cinchona. You'll have another episode in about two days. Much milder if you stay on these tablets." He eyed her shrewdly. "But I'm not sure you'll take them as directed."

"Why wouldn't I?"

He wondered whether to talk about his diagnosis, and decided to approach it by indirection. "Are you happy?"

"Oh, famously. Ah can hardly wait to be up and rarin'."

"I can hardly imagine a woman in your position being very happy. You're far from home, I take it."

"Ah sure am. War's upsettin' everyone in the whole parish."

"Well, you escaped the war, only to fall into your own type of slavery."

"Whatevah are you sayin'?"

"Well, Mister Ace...he told me you'd taken up with a riverboat gambler and come west with him, and then he wagered a great deal of money...ah, over ten thousand dollars...for you."

"Oh, my, Ah could hardly stand it."

"Yes, that's the point. Just so. You had no say in the matter. Here were two uncaring gamblers wagering for the possession of a beautiful woman."

"Yoah a dear, callin' me that, especially how I look now. But that's why Ah could hardly stand it! Ah never dreamed Ah was worth ten thousand dollars."

That took the doctor aback. Could this gentle Southern belle be just as barbarous as her consorts? He leaned forward a bit. "I believe your gentleman is asleep in the parlor. We can talk freely. I think you're in desperate circumstances, far from home, alone, with no future, desolate. I think you opened your arms and embraced the ague hoping it would deliver you from your mortal coil. I think you weep inside, even while you smile to the world."

"Ah sure was sick," she said, a smile building on that gorgeous, ravaged face.

"Yes. And sometimes sickness is caused by despair. The spirit within us says to the body, let go of life, and the body lets go." He paused pregnantly. "That's the case, isn't it, Rosa?"

"Whatevah are you sayin'?"

"Everything's been taken from you. Your natural liberty, your woman's dignity. Men wager for you. There's nothing left. Not sweet motherhood, not respectability, not life in the bosom of your family raising sweet children. It's all gone."

"Yoah crack-brained. Where'd you say you come from?"

"I'm Hungarian. I learnt English studying surgery a year in Edinburgh, under Lister, after my schooling in Hungary."

"Well, you listen to me, Doctor Gallups. Ah never did have such a thrill in my life. Getting' bet on for ten thousand Yankee dollars! Woo-ee!"

It was dawning on Sandor Gollancz that he had misdiagnosed the case. "Tell me," he said quietly, "what you want in life?"

"Why, Ah just will, honey. When Billy's bank fattens up a bit, we're goin' to Virginia City, and Ah'll deal and we'll see who bets on me. Ah'd just love to be worth fifty thousand dollars. Billy thinks I'm worth it. Why, Ah've had ambition since I was a girl."

Gollancz stared at her, incredulous. "But what if you didn't like the gentleman who won you?"

"Why, Ah'd ask him to bet me for a hundred thousand. Ah'd just love to be won by one of those Silver Kings, like Mackey or Fair, or some San Francisco gold king."

"But what of your personal life?"

"That is my personal life! If I got wagered at a hundred thousand dollars there'd be nobody on earth...nobody...who'd ever snub me again!"

"But...." The doctor's protestation faded in his throat. He wanted to know whether her liberty meant a thing to her. It didn't seem to. These crass Americans talked a lot about it, but chased money and kept slaves. "What if you refused to live with the man who'd won you on a wager?"

"Ah just might," she said. "Then they'd call me the woman who cost some old fool a hundred thousand dollars. That'd be just as nice."

"But what of love?" Gollancz asked weakly.

"Why, you old goose, what's a better pledge of love than a hundred thousand dollars? Ah'd be so flattered Ah'd just wrap my arms around that little old man and kiss him to death."

Gollancz had an awful urge to try an eleven thousand bet for her, but he didn't have a thousand to his name. He eyed the voluptuous Rosa, all too aware of the way the damp cotton clung to her perfect curves.

"I've seen you through," he said abruptly. "I'm a bit weary myself." He counted out thirty tablets from the pasteboard box. "I want you to take one of these every eight hours," he said. "Have you taken quinine before?"

"Oh, a few times."

"Then you know there'll be several attacks, each one weaker. This is enough for ten days. Drink a lot of water. If the fever comes back, send for me. If your urine is black or discolored, send for me."

"Yoah a dear."

"No, I'm a man without a country," he said. "Shall I leave a statement with you?"

"Oh, stick Billy with it."

Dr. Gollancz pulled his nib and ink bottle and statement pad from the Gladstone, and charged Billy seven dollars for the long consultation and vigil, and two-fifty for the quinine. He doubted he would ever be paid. He placed the bill on a table in the parlor and peered around, wondering what the place would tell him. Not the slightest effort had gone into beautifying the little flat. Cheap furniture filled it. Not a lithograph or painting graced a wall. No carpet softened the plank floor. This wasn't a home; it was a nesting place. No one in the American West had a home.

The doctor padded past the gambler, who snored on the sofa, and softly let himself out. When he reached the street, he found it gilded by the horizontal sun. He stood there and stretched, enjoying the velvety dry air, and the hush that would soon vanish under the frenetic labor of the Americans. He meant to nap a few hours.

These Americans! Barbarous! A woman whose self-esteem was based on the amount someone might gamble to have her! A man who'd wagered his last cent to win her! He laughed. He didn't mind it at all. Truth to tell, he wished he had the brass to live like that. He thought he would if he stayed here. He himself was changing. This fierce, rocky, harsh land was somehow transforming him into a man who matched the desert. He had intended to sow a few wild oats for a few years and then sail for Le Havre, having had his fill of American wildness. But this morning he knew he wouldn't. He would never have his fill of this reckless people and this new land.

HEARTS

Laura Duvall had expected every man in Tombstone to wear a sidearm, but that was not what she discovered as the Wells Fargo agent opened the door of her coach. She did not see a holstered weapon. At least not at first.

She had choked on the golden dust all the way from Benson, along with the fumes emanating from seven over-heated males jammed onto the sticky leather seats. She knew the Arizona heat would torment her, and had prepared for it as best she could with a dress of white muslin that filtered air through her gauzy camisole and petticoat.

It was her turn to step out, and as she did so, she spotted a familiar face in the shadow of the awning over the boardwalk. John Behan, sheriff of Tombstone. She knew him but he didn't know her. She would have known him even without the polished steel circlet on his chest. She had studied numerous tintypes of him and had read lengthy reports describing him. One thing he always did was meet the stage.

And now he was lounging casually in the shadow, out of the fierce Arizona sun this May day of 1881. She stepped into the dust of Allen Street and let the faint breeze begin to erase the sweat that had darkened the armpits of her white dress. Behan's attention was entirely upon her. She did that to certain men. She was not particularly beautiful, but striking, with bold chestnut hair now largely concealed under her broad-brimmed white straw hat. She turned her back to Behan, a deliberate gesture fraught with messages. The jehu and Wells Fargo agent were unloading the boot, where her two items of luggage nestled.

Duvall was not her real name, but she used it with some success in her field, where French names opened doors. It had been the name of her lover, Jean Duvall. The late Jean Duvall, but few people knew that, either. Before that she had been married to a dull Army lieutenant, Jason Keogh, but he had divorced her... for adultery.

She bent her thoughts away from that. Her two pieces of luggage descended to the dirt of the street. One was a routine pebbled black leather portmanteau; the other a curious oblong case that always aroused curiosity. It held the oilcloth faro layout, the faro box, case keeper, numerous unopened decks of plain-backed cards, and several chip trays.

She eyed the luggage, knowing she would need a porter, and that's when Behan glided in.

"Help you, ma'am?"

The sheriff stood before her, darkly Irish, of medium height, a man with knowing eyes and a face full of question marks and lust.

"Why, you're the sheriff. Perhaps you can recommend a hotel."

His gaze surveyed her and she understood that he was not merely assessing the obvious costliness of her attire. He had instantly discovered the thing she tried so hard to conceal, the thing that only a connoisseur of women would unearth. Not even her high-necked and prim dress could conceal her vulnerability from eyes such as his. He had known nothing about her, but suddenly knew everything.

That figured. Sheriff Behan was a Democrat. Laura Duvall had formulated an iron law of life: Republican gents were bad lovers but were good at business, while Democrat males knew everything there is to know about pleasing a woman but couldn't do anything else with their feckless lives. John Behan was a case in point. She knew that in five minutes he would turn her to pudding, and that he was dangerous, and that she must avoid him and get on with her mission.

"The Cosmopolitan Hotel, I think. It would be suitable for a lady of your sort."

"Thank you. You may take my bags there," she said, faintly enjoying the imperial command.

"And whom do I have the honor of welcoming to town?"

"Laura Duvall," she said.

His eyes registered nothing.

"I am Sheriff Behan, at your service," he said.

"No doubt about it," she said.

He plucked up her bags, obviously curious about the oblong one. "What do you do?" he asked.

"Gamble."

"A lady gambler. Well, I know a few parlors where you'd be welcome."

"I am rarely unwelcome."

He steered her into the hotel, which stood only a few doors away, and waited while she negotiated a room.

"You're in luck," he said. "Usually it's full. It's not the cheapest place in town, either."

He was fishing. She smiled.

"Thank you, Mister Behan. I'm sure we'll be running into each other soon."

Behan stood there, trying to prolong the meeting, but finally smiled and retreated into the heat.

The clerk helped her to her second-floor room.

Her expense money from William was adequate, but it wouldn't allow her to stay in this sort of quarters for long unless she got very lucky. The Pinkertons did not pay their agents well. He had sent her here to find out what she could about the rampant lawlessness in Cochise County. He had wanted a detailed telegraphic report in a fortnight, if possible. They had worked out a code and an address that would keep the report and its recipient entirely private.

Somebody wanted to untie the Gordian knots of Cochise County, but William refused to tell her who his client was.

"It's best if you don't know. Keep an open mind. Look at all sides. Use your charms."

She knew what he had meant.

"Each side is pointing fingers at the other. All we know is that rustling is rampant...murder so commonplace that it is scarcely noted in the local papers...and Wells Fargo coaches carrying bullion from the silver mines are robbed so frequently that the losses for the insurers, Wells Fargo, and the mines, are rocketing. Death is in the air down there."

"It's Wells Fargo, then."

"I'm not at liberty to say, and don't assume anything. I will tell you one thing...Wells Fargo already has a private agent in Tombstone."

And that was all she could get out of him.

This would be rather easy. She would report to William in a fortnight, maybe less. Women had their ways. She already knew the cast of characters, thanks to some elaborate preparation in the Chicago offices of the Pinkerton Detective Agency. All she needed was to start some pillow talk.

She doffed her muslin dress, poured water from the pitcher into the bowl, and gave herself a spit-bath. The tepid water felt like heaven. Twenty minutes later she was ready for Tombstone. With luck, she might have her game going before nightfall.

Odd how she already liked the town even before examining it closely. It had the effrontery to put on cosmopolitan airs, even if it had mushroomed out of desert wastes in barely three years. It was all veneer, like the flocked blood-red wallpaper that hid the rude planks of this ramshackle building. It was a gaudy fake of a burg, and reminded her of herself.

She liked Johnny Behan, and wished she didn't. What sort of man met the arriving coaches just to womanize? She liked to be womanized, and that was the trouble. The Pinkertons didn't know that.

Like most Arizona towns, this one slumbered through the midday heat. Tonight it would come alive and kill a few more people. She didn't like daylight anyway. But she would have to brave the sun now, and try to set herself up.

She finished her ablutions, dabbed lilac between her breasts, and headed into the blistering heat. Her objective was the Oriental, less than a block away, the best saloon and gambling emporium in Tombstone, and the locus of high rollers. Wyatt Earp had a piece of the action there. Lou Rickabaugh, Dick Clark, and Bill Harris ran the gambling operation, and had given Earp a quarter interest mainly to protect the place. The other side, the Cowboys and Behan, were scheming to shut it down.

Earp was a Republican, damn him. He wouldn't know the first thing about women and, worse, wouldn't care.

She walked through the open double doors and into gloom. Her first impression of the Oriental was one of ornate melancholia. A gorgeous mahogany and white marble bar dominated one side. Light from the front doors faded swiftly, and to the rear, where the solemn gambling tables lay, the darkness was pervasive. But she could make out a handsome blue and gold Brussels carpet, and extravagant glass chandeliers above. At night it would be different, but by day the Oriental was as forlorn as a cemetery. The place was almost empty, which was what she expected midafternoon of a weekday.

The rank odor of smelly armpits told her men were about somewhere in there. She made out assorted bodies once her eyes adjusted. Only one table was operating, a faro outfit with a small dim lamp burning above it. It had no customers.

But closer at hand, at a marble bar table, sat several dead-faced men she identified at once, again from assorted tintypes she had scrutinized. Wyatt Earp and his brother Morgan. Lou Rickabaugh. Dapper Luke Short, looking like a Manhattan swell but far more deadly. They were sipping fizzy phosphates.

Good.

"You looking for something, ma'am?" The sepulchral voice emanated from the mustachioed bartender she knew to be Frank Leslie, an enigmatic gunman. Was it the faint redolence of burnt gunpowder that stamped the Oriental as the most memorable sporting palace she had ever been in?

"Yes, the owners of the gambling concession."

The bartender nodded her toward the sole occupied table.

Rickabaugh stood.

"You come to reform Tombstone, ma'am?"

"I deal."

"No women," said Wyatt Earp.

She stared at the Illinois man. Big, slim, blond, ice-blue eyes, and a gaze that would frost a windowpane. He stared back, his eyes measuring her for God knows what. Probably a black enameled coffin. He was not visibly heeled. Her pulse quickened. What was it about him?

"That's a little quick," she said. "I bring trade."

"Women are trouble."

She turned to portly, graying Rickabaugh. "I'm Linda Duvall. I'll improve your trade. Do you want profits or not?"

Earp remained quiet this time.

"We don't need anyone, Miss Duvall."

"Missus."

"Ah, yes, but recently widowed. New Orleans, right?"

She nodded.

"Aw, Wyatt, we need some action," said Morgan, admiring her with a bedroom stare. He oozed youthful enthusiasm and she wondered how long he let his cautious older brother dominate him.

"We've some safety concerns," Rickabaugh said. "If Mister Earp is not inclined to let you run a table, then I'll have to acquiesce, as much as I'd be inclined to try out so comely a lady."

She didn't dislike him.

Wyatt continued to stare. "No women in here, but I'll buy you a sarsaparilla," he said. "Then you'll take your trade elsewhere."

Rickabaugh looked unhappy but said no more.

"I made a temperance oath. No lips that touch sarsaparilla will ever touch mine. You sure you won't change your mind?"

Morgan snickered.

Wyatt never answered, but turned to the others. They had been discussing the recent perforation of some tinhorn called Charlie Storms by Luke Short, and returned to it. The perfume of gunpowder was what seduced Earps. They never noticed the cologne between her breasts.

She stood on one foot and then the other, but the employment interview had terminated. That damned Wyatt Earp.

No women.

She hurried out. The dead heat slapped her. She headed across Fourth Street and plunged into the Crystal Palace, and found it better lit from side windows. It boasted a made-in-France brass and porcelain chandelier, chased brass spittoons, and a gaudy cherry wood bar with a fat lady, naked save for a diaphanous something or other crawling over her thick thighs, gazing down from a gilt frame.

She approached the keep, a mustachioed bald spaniel with pop eyes.

"Who runs the games?"

"We don't serve women," the keep said.

"I said who runs the games? I deal."

"Forget it. He don't allow women behind the tables. You want to play, that's O.K. You want to deal, you go down the street."

"I'll come back and ask him tonight."

The keep shrugged.

What the hell. Tombstone was a man's world.

She knew better than to try Jim Earp's Sampling Room, so she headed along Allen to the Alhambra, and got the same story. No distaff dealers. They once let Poker Annie play a high stakes game for fifty-one hours, but she was so ugly no one got into a fight, the keep explained.

She did no better at the Occidental. In fact, worse. The slick-haired tinhorn told her to set up shop in the sporting district. She could run a game there.

"I may be a sporting lady," she said, "but not on my back. I deal sitting up."

"You can sport with me sitting up," he said.

She was used to it.

They were all as bad as the Earps. Tombstone had no room for women. For the first time since she arrived, she began to fret about her mission. Her employer wanted facts. If she couldn't siphon them off the gaming tables, she would have to think of something else. But what?

She hiked back to the Cosmopolitan, wanting to lick her wounds and think. Bill Pinkerton had given her a couple of small jobs, but this was her first big one, and she didn't want to disappoint him.

She had known the Pinkertons for years. Family friends. She had grown up in flossy circles on Chicago's north shore, the daughter of a Great Lakes steamboat magnate. She had been given everything a young lady could want, and had made her debut to introduce her to polite society and potential husbands.

But she wasn't made for polite society. They had called her brazen and reckless back then, and several swain backed out of marriages at the eleventh hour. She couldn't help it. She had no intention of being the mistress of some dull brick pile on Lake Michigan full of whining children.

So much happened, so fast, that she could barely remember the whirligig. She had gotten herself disinherited after one wild episode, married an Army captain during one of her occasional respectable interludes, found herself divorced and in bed with a New Orleans gambler, and learned the trade only to have him succumb to a lead pill that erupted from a rival's Derringer. Then she was on her own, and that was when William Pinkerton, who knew her well and had kept track, recruited her.

"Laura," he said, "you're perfect for us. At home in any situation. At home in a mansion or a yacht, at home in a casino, at home with the demimonde. At home with any sort of man."

The latter had been said delicately. Her conquests were legend. She had permitted herself a wry smile. Sleuthing would be entertaining, and being entertained was more important than money, except when she had none. She planned to give Bill Pinkerton about a hundred times his money's worth.

Her treatment at the Oriental rankled. If Wyatt Earp had the slightest understanding of the ways of the world, he would have shown her some respect. From her very first glance she had known she would do anything, be anything, for Wyatt Earp, and she loathed herself for it.

She knew that the worse he treated her, the harder she would try to seduce him. She knew all about him. He had stolen some theatrical tramp named Josie Marcus from Sheriff Behan, and that was one of the reasons Tombstone smoldered. A Juliet was usually at the bottom of gang wars, and Tombstone was about to be torn apart by one.

She intended to knock Wyatt Earp down a few pegs, and maybe the way to do it was already at hand. She had caught the eye of the sheriff, and that was an ace of hearts.

Much to her surprise, Sheriff Behan was sitting there in the small lobby. He rose smoothly as she entered.

"Ah, it's Miss Duvall. How did it go?"

"I think you already know."

He smiled. The man was as smooth as baby flesh. "Lawmen do hear things," he said. "It seems our sporting establishments have no room for a lady."

"A woman, you mean. Whether I'm a lady is debatable."

"A lady," he said. "It's a man's town, all right. How did matters proceed at the Oriental?"

"Mister Wyatt B.S. Earp would have no part of me."

"How do you know his middle initials?"

"I live in the sporting world."

He smiled again. *Butter lips*, she thought. "Perhaps you are better off not working there."

"Why?"

"Oh, the Earps are not appreciated in some quarters."

"Your quarters."

He smiled once again. He was the smilingest sheriff she had ever met.

"You have something against him," she said. *Like an actress named Josie.*

His smile retreated for a moment. "I will help you if you wish."

"Maybe."

"Come along. I'll talk with certain friends at the Crystal Palace. I'll tell them that a woman dealer is good for trade. You'll suck the players right out of Rickabaugh's place, a looker like you. What shall I offer? You run your own table and they get a quarter of your take? That's the usual."

She nodded. The man had been around.

It took only moments. Behan talked to the proprietor, a man named Frank, and Frank talked to her, and she nodded, and she was invited to set up her table in a place that reminded her of a New Orleans mortuary.

"Give the Oriental a little competition," Frank said.

"There you are, Missus Duvall. A table and a living. You may thank me by letting me take you to dinner at the Maison Dore. Fine food, best this side of San Francisco."

She agreed. Behan didn't waste a minute.

"You gonna start tonight?" Frank asked.

"Don't copper the bet," she replied.

The gaudy French restaurant astonished her. Johnny Behan astonished her, too. It would cost him a week's salary to feed her there. Plainly, wearing the badge was a lucrative business.

She waited until they were knife-deep in filets mignons before opening up certain lines of inquiry.

"I don't think I like Wyatt Earp," she said.

"So I heard."

"Then you already know the story. We don't want women, he said, and that was it. I was dealt out."

"That's what I heard."

"You have funnels for ears. Come on, Johnny Behan, tell me who runs Tombstone."

He smiled again, as if life were a secret.

They drifted through four courses, but not until the chocolate mousse did Sheriff Behan pitch the deal.

"You need protection," he said. "Single woman. I'll make sure you're unharmed and free to run your game for one quarter of the take...."

She smiled and awaited the rest. A man like Behan would give her options.

Two spoonfuls of mousse later he offered her the rest.

"Of course, you could always live with me."

"Pay you your quarter? And pay that Frank his quarter? And pay Cochise County and Tombstone taxes for my table? That's another quarter. So I keep about a quarter of my winnings? That'd break the bank. The odds are no good."

"I am very skilled at what I do," he said softly.

She turned into pudding.

"I will decide after looking at your rooms and I hear the rest of your offer."

He nodded.

He led her through dead desert dusk to Toughnut Street, where he maintained a small shiplap-sided cottage with spindle gingerbread. That was luxury in a boom town like Tombstone. Within, she discovered lace curtains on each window, doilies strewn promiscuously over the horsehair furniture, a bathing closet with a clawfoot tub, sink, and running water, and an unused dead kitchen with a zinc sink. The bedroom contained a single four-poster marital bed with a bedpan under it. A privy stood at the rear corner of the lot.

"Well?"

"Where is my bed?"

"You get me in the bargain."

She laughed, not unhappily. "I don't sell myself."

"My cut for protecting you is one fourth...unless you move in. You move in and there's no game table taxes, either. You keep everything except for Frank's cut."

Damn him. Damn him. He had ferreted her out and he was right. "All right, I'll try it. We'll see. Don't count on anything. Move my stuff from the hotel. I'm going to deal tonight, and after that, I'll be here."

He wasn't going to see her in this room again until two or three in the morning.

"I will do that," he said.

She had her table running by nine. A crowd gathered to buck the tiger — and have a gander. She invited the gander with a *décolleté* neckline. The players stood three deep, and she was reaping a fat profit as she pulled the turns out of the faro box. At times, she saw Behan gazing her way. At other times, she discovered various Earps, especially Wyatt, peering dead-eyed at her and her spectacular trade. The gents from the Oriental didn't look a bit happy.

A shrewd jowly player, probably another tinhorn, kept doubling on his losses until she pointed at the sign saying there was a twenty-five-dollar limit, and then he got angry and began baiting her. Behan materialized out of nowhere.

"You heard the lady," he said.

The player turned and found himself staring at the steel circlet. He withdrew fifteen one-dollar blue chips, leaving twenty-five, and won on a coppered seven. He was still behind, but picked up his money and retreated, still under Behan's steady gaze.

Laura Duvall sighed.

In the dead of the night she discovered the sheriff was as much a killer in bed as a lady's man, and that was going to ruin her judgment. Damn Democrat Johnny Behan all to hell.

That's how it went. But she learned nothing of consequence, except the names of those who came to visit Sheriff Behan. Whatever they said, they said far from her ears. Even so, the events of the next weeks bore out what information the Pinkertons already had: Behan's associates, the "Cowboys", were a mob of reckless outlaws from the adjoining ranches. The Clanton boys, the McLaury boys, John Ringo, Curly Bill Brocius, a dozen more hard and murderous men. They all smiled politely at her, if she happened to be around, and led the sheriff off into the dusty streets. Behan spent a lot of time talking in a dead whisper to Harry Wood, editor of *The Nugget*, the Democrat paper that loudly defended them and Sheriff Behan, and assailed the Earps and John Henry Holliday, known as Doc.

It dawned on her that the odds were staggering. The Earp brothers, and Holliday, and maybe a couple others, against a dizzying mob of fifty or sixty, every one of them skilled with deadly weapons, full of brag, and without even the tatters of conscience.

Boozy Harry Wood made every effort to lay the blame for ongoing hold-ups, stagecoach robberies, rustling, and mayhem at the door of the Earps, while Mayor John Clum's Republican *Epitaph* returned the fire, but less effectually. The Cowboys spent their ill-gotten loot liberally, and made friends everywhere, especially in the cathouses.

She heard talk of murder, revenge, triumph.

So they were going to kill the Earps and throw Holliday's emaciated corpse to the dogs. It was all coming clear. There were badges enough all around: the Earps had a deputy federal marshal badge and a city marshal badge. The Cowboys had a sheriff's badge. Legal murder.

The novelty of a woman faro dealer drew a lusty crowd every night. As word got around the moribund outlying ranches, players drifted to the Crystal Palace and stood three deep at her table, waiting for the chance to play. That pleased her. She was bleeding trade from the Oriental, and making Wyatt Earp rue his words. A striking lady with a low neckline drew more players than some grease-haired tinhorn with soiled cuffs and tobacco-stained teeth.

Johnny Behan hovered around in the background, his meaty presence discouraging the toughs from trying to snatch her bank or cheat her or bully her with fake grievances. No sooner had a fortnight passed than the Crystal Palace was the hottest gambling emporium in Tombstone, every night a wake. She opened at three in the afternoon and rarely closed up before two in the morning, and the afternoons were her only slow moments.

That's when a woman named Kate drifted in and began playing during the sunlit afternoons when no one else was around. Laura liked her looks. Kate had a magnificent nose, thin and long and prominent, curved like a raptor's beak, an eagle nose, a noble nose that made her look royal. She spoke with a subtle accent that Laura discovered was Hungarian.

"I am John Henry Holliday's lover," Kate said one afternoon. "I have come to tell you things."

"Tell me?" Something froze in Laura. Had she been uncovered?

"I will tell you for my own reasons, even if you are Johnny Behan's woman."

"Why tell me anything? Keep your own counsel. If it's anything against Johnny, I don't want to hear it."

"Johnny is a famous lover. Not like the Earps."

Kate played a chip on a king, and Laura drew a turn. The king lost.

"Don't ever got hooked up with the Earps," she said. "At least not Wyatt. He uses women and throws them out."

"I have no intention. And why don't you talk about something else?"

"Because Wyatt is looking at you. He comes over here and watches you and thinks you don't notice."

"Mostly I don't. I keep my eyes on the board. You can't run a faro game any other way."

"What Johnny Behan has, Wyatt wants. He stole his Josie from Behan and kicked out his poor drunken Mattie. Now he's going to steal you."

Laura smiled. "Is this what you came to warn me about?"

"Yes. And not to believe a word, not one word, that Johnny Behan says about Doc or any of them."

Kate peered about sharply, afraid she had been overheard. She put five chips on the eight and coppered it. Laura drew a king and a four and adjusted the cases. Kate let her bet ride.

"Come to me if you want to know anything," Kate said. "I know everything."

Laura's caution welled up again. "About what?"

"About anything."

Laura yawned, drew a seven and six, and shuffled the deck, pulled the soda and hock and laid them face up under the deck, and placed it in the faro box. Then she adjusted the cases and awaited Kate's play.

Laura kept her curiosity in check. "The only thing that interests me is my game," she said.

"Not Johnny?"

"It's cheaper than the Cosmopolitan...and paying the cut he wanted."

"So is Doc's room."

They laughed.

"What's Doc like?" Laura asked.

"A Southern gentleman, fragile, sad, quick-tempered, and self-obsessed because consumption is killing him. He uses me. But I love him and always have. Is that strange?"

"No, not strange. Is he solvent?"

"Almost always. Cards are a living. He can't practice dentistry any more. Not with consumption. But when he's broke, that's what he does until he's got a new stake."

"Why do the Cowboys say he robbed a stagecoach?"

"He's too sick to rob a child of candy. I beg of you, don't listen to Johnny Behan."

"Why does Johnny Behan say it, then?"

"Because Wyatt Earp stole that slut actress from him, and Doc is a friend of the Earps."

Laura smiled and cleaned Kate's five chips off the board. She had drawn a pair of eights, and all ties went to the house.

Kate sighed, and vanished toward the blind-bright doorway and the Crystal Palace went dead.

With a little encouragement, Doc Holliday's woman would divulge much of what Laura needed to know.

The next day Wyatt Earp sat down at her table, hulking over it as if he owned it. He had obviously waited for the moment when no other players were around. He exuded a faint malice, and she found herself loathing him. He bought a stack of dollar chips, laid one on the deuce, and coppered it.

She shuffled the deck, pulled the soda and hock, and stuffed it into the faro box. The first turn produced a seven and two. She pulled the chip off the table.

"You're costing us business," he said.

"That's good to know."

"What would it take to get you to leave?"

"I'm happy where I am."

If she had disliked him before, she hated him now. The man was a cool, assessing bully.

"You're Behan's lady."

She reddened slightly. "You're wrong on both counts."

He ignored it. "You're Behan's spy. Everything said at this table siphons into his big Irish ears, along with all your winnings."

"I'm glad you think so," she said. "And if I am, what's it to you? Here's Laura Duvall, setting up shop in the Crystal Palace because Wyatt Earp didn't want her in the Oriental. Here's Duvall, ending up with Sheriff Behan because Wyatt Earp wouldn't let her make an honest living in Tombstone. I tried every saloon in town and they all said no, and now I know why. Virgil made threats."

"You'd better be on the next stage out of town."

"I knew I was going to despise you. Play, dammit. Only players sit at my table."

"It doesn't matter to me what women think."

"Oh? Is that so? What I think is that Sheriff Behan's a crook. He lives pretty high on a sheriff salary, and I can't say I admire the gang he runs with. The only thing good about him is his way with women. He's a Democrat, and Democrats know how to pleasure ladies. I've yet to meet a Republican who was any good at it. He's a better man than you."

That sure as hell froze Deputy U.S. Marshal Earp to his stool.

"Still want me to leave?"

"Yes."

"Just try it."

He grinned suddenly and unexpectedly. "Maybe I will."

"You're a son-of-a-bitch, Wyatt Earp."

Earp drifted into silence. A poxed cowboy, actually one of

Behan's crowd, settled down, bought some chips, and began playing.

"I'll cash these," said Earp. "Cowshit's pretty thick around here."

She gave him eleven dollars.

That's how it stood. She was about to be booted out of Tombstone before she could finish her task. William Pinkerton was getting impatient. He'd spent a lot to put her in place, and she hadn't given him one snippet of information. The coded wires grew tart.

In the month she'd spent in Tombstone, it had all become clear enough. The Earps were brutes and greedy, but basically law-abiding and supported by the town's merchants. The Cowboys were flat-out badmen, itchy with the trigger finger, crooks, grafters, rustlers, stagecoach robbers, and ferocious executioners who didn't hesitate to rob and kill people in lonely places. The Cowboys were more fun. Behan milked the county of all it was worth, and raked off a percentage of the gang's take, in exchange for "protection".

One other thing was obvious: the Earps, and their handful, were outnumbered about ten to one, and weren't long for this world. Every time Laura spotted Wyatt or Morgan or Virgil Earp, she knew she was observing a dead man. Any day, something would set off the whole thing, and the Earp brothers would occupy permanent addresses on Boot Hill.

Young Morgan Earp played her game now and then, mostly to look down her neck, but Virgil never sat down and Wyatt played only to see who was buying her chips. She never saw the Earp women and wouldn't have recognized them if they had walked in. Wyatt Earp fascinated her, and stirred something morbid in her belly she couldn't name. He used women, Kate had told her, and there was something in Laura willing to be used. He drew women to him but would be a lousy lover. That was his paradox. It really didn't matter. Sometime, unless the Earps packed up, they would be lying cold and pickled in that glass-walled hearse that paraded down Allen Street a couple times a week.

She encountered Doc Holliday only once or twice, and knew that he wasn't long for the world, either. Death lay in his gaze, and if consumption didn't take him soon, he would try to hasten the matter by provoking a quarrel of his own. But she could see why her friend Kate, with the big nose, put such store in him. That frail, tragic honor-bound man was like a bird with a broken wing.

Then the kid, Morgan, quit playing at her table, and then Virgil began nabbing patrons of the Crystal Palace for public drunkenness and fining them eleven dollars. Then they announced a cockamamie new rule: no women in saloons. Laura knew it was aimed dead square at her, and it was because she was cleaning up. She had taken half the trade away from the Oriental, and the Earps finally decided to do something about it.

"You're my protector, so do something," she said to Johnny.

"I don't enforce city ordinances, Laura. I can't. I'm a county officer. It's up to Virgil Earp."

"So tell the Earps to get the hell out of the way."

He stared at her, and she realized he was dead afraid of them. Johnny the Protector wasn't protecting her.

"Guess I'll move on," she said. "Frank says I got to pack up the game and never come back to the Palace."

"No, stay."

"It's called whoring."

"What is?"

"My favors for your support. No thanks. I've got better things to do. I like the action."

"Suit yourself."

That was dead-hearted Johnny Behan, for you.

She packed up her rig at the Crystal Palace, paid Frank his quarter of the last night's deadfall, and stepped across the clay of Fifth Street and into the Oriental.

"You're not supposed to be in here," said Bill Harris.

"I won't be long. Where's the iceberg?"

"The who?"

"Wyatt."

"Taking lunch at his brother's saloon."

That meant crossing Allen Street, which she did, managing not to dip her hem in manure.

He was in there.

"Don't tell me I can't be in here, damn you."

He shrugged. Virgil, off in a corner, started to get up.

"I'll deal for you in the Oriental," she said. "Quit putting women out of saloons and I'll earn you more money than you ever saw before."

For once, that damned Wyatt Earp smiled. She didn't know how it was possible because he lacked the proper facial muscles.

"No. You should get out of here."

"Why?"

Earp peered about. A pair of rummies sat at the far end of the bar, talking to each other. He turned his back to them and lowered his voice.

"Because William wants you to."

She froze. "What are you talking about?"

"You stayed too long. They want the report. You should have wired it two weeks ago."

"You don't make any sense," she said, fearing that he made all too much sense.

"William Pinkerton asked us to boot you out of Tombstone."

"Wyatt Earp, you think you know something but you don't."

"You did a good job. Got right in bed with the Democrats."

She reddened.

"Miss Duvall, sweetheart, did you imagine that Republican President Garfield, would hire the Republican Pinkertons, to look into some political rivalry in the Territory without knowing in advance which side to support? Did you think they were going to turn their backs on the Republican Earps?"

She absorbed that. "I was working for the Garfield administration?"

"You sure were. They'd heard Tombstone was getting a bit frolicsome, and the President thought to run in the Army or something. But first they needed facts. They turned to your Chicago friends to get them."

"And?"

"William sent you hither."

"And?"

"Instructed us to make sure you set up in the right shop. The Oriental isn't the right place. We hardly see a Cowboy in there. So we had to nudge you a little. Push you into the arms of Johnny Behan. Get you a table in a Cowboy hang-out. Get you out of Tombstone when you overstayed."

"And?"

"It worked fine. Go wire your report. You know exactly who's rustling and robbing and killing around here. William's going to be pleased with it. Then catch the next train East."

It angered her. William Pinkerton had set up the whole deal. The President would get a report he could put to good use.

"You look unhappy...Jimmy, give her a sarsaparilla."

"The hell with you, Wyatt Earp," she said.

He laughed. "Have a drink."

"It was a sham. The whole thing was a sham. William sent me down here for nothing."

"No, for something. He could truthfully tell the President he had an operative here and she had laid the troubles to the Cowboys."

She had never been angrier. Swiftly, she came to some decisions. That swine William Pinkerton wouldn't get a report from her. Not one damned word. In fact he would never see her again. And she wasn't returning to Chicago. She'd head for Leadville and set up her game. The big play in Tombstone had supplied her with a fat bank, two thousand dollars. She'd take on the high rollers up in Colorado, and enjoy it. Johnny Behan, crook and grafter that he was, had treated her with ten times more respect.

She smiled suddenly. "You've got one thing wrong, Wyatt. I've been in bed with Republicans."

THE BUSINESS OF DYING

Homer Winslow knew that they were going to plant him at the age of twenty-four. He lay in his tent thinking about that, mournful, desolated by the unfairness of it. But he couldn't escape it, short of a miracle. The weakness oppressed him. They called it the stomach complaint, and a lot of the men grubbing gold out of the gulches of the Sierras had succumbed to it.

No one had a cure for him, nor were there doctors or hospitals in California, though he'd heard that plenty of physicians had come West with the rest of the Forty-Niners. The doctors would call it dysentery, but that was too fancy a name for the polyglot gold grubbers clawing nuggets and dust out of all the bars and branches of the American River. All Homer knew was that the complaint was a mortifying, demeaning, cruel, and undignified way to shuck his mortal coil. Every time he crawled for the bushes, a breathtaking hurt and weakness and dizziness overwhelmed him.

He had tried every cure his rough colleagues had recommended. Even though vegetables were nigh impossible to get, he had bought some, following the advice of those sages who said he'd do better once he varied the salt pork and beans. Others had condemned coffee or tea, while others insisted that he take not the slightest drop of ardent spirits. Still others insisted that he eat fish only, and never a slice of red meat. One fellow, a Wisconsin farmer before he came West in the rush, told Homer to try salt. What was needed, he explained, was something with an affinity to water, that would lock water in Winslow's desperately dehydrated and weakened body.

Nothing worked. He would have liked to go on down to the great tent city of Sacramento for help, thinking maybe the rough conditions of the mountains, or the thinner air, was at fault. He even dreamed of continuing to that other tent city, San Francisco, where, surely, he could find a competent surgeon. But he was too far gone. He would never survive the trip, strapped to the top of some freight wagon, or handed onto the deck of one of the great steamers plying the river trade.

Each day his strength ebbed, and he knew the end would come soon. He had lost hope. His mind was clear, even though his body suffered waves of cold and nausea that gripped him and twisted his guts. The men of Mad Mule Gulch had actually been tender, and he could ask nothing more. Homer had a good gravel claim, a foot to bedrock, ten feet wide and stretching from bank to bank, according to the miner's law for that locale. He had left his tools there, the inviolable mark of a claim, and no one had jumped it. Even better, should any stranger try to jump it, every gold-grubbing man in the gulch would deal swiftly with the interloper.

Even kinder was Homer's tent mate, Phineas Parsons. They had met here, formed a partnership as was the custom, and helped each other. Phineas never abandoned Homer. He prepared the daily broth that Homer managed to swallow, and even washed Homer's soiled clothing. But Phineas's kindest act was to devote an hour a day to Homer's fine claim, usually panning out an ounce of gold for Homer, which bought necessaries. Before the complaint took him, Homer had grubbed almost nine hundred dollars of flaky gold, with an occasional nugget as a bonus. This he kept in a lidded butter crock beside his head.

No one would steal it. No sensible miner ever stole. It was live and let live on the western slope of the Sierras, and swift, merciless justice for those who violated the code. But things were changing. Whole shiploads of Australians, mostly convicts shipped out from England, were arriving in the camps, bent on looting and pillaging. And Homer had heard there were even pigtailed Chinamen and Chileans flooding in, galvanized by the awesome news from Sutter's Mill, though he had never seen any of them.

Dusk came, and Homer sensed the cessation of toil around Mad Mule Bar. Twilight fell earlier and earlier these autumnal days, and soon winter would chase the miners out of the mountains. Most would flee to San Francisco or Sacramento, and try the fandango with *señoritas*, or drink some of the whiskey shipped in plentiful amounts around the horn. But not Homer. He would not be leaving the mountains this time.

He heard Phineas rustling about outside the tent, smelled smoke, and knew his partner was starting the cook fire. Presently Phineas poked his bearded face into the darkened interior.

"You all right, Homer?" he asked.

"No."

"Getting worse?"

"I'm done for."

"You figuring on heading for the other shore?"

"Day or two."

"Wish I could help. Don't know how in tarnation to help."

"There's no way."

Phineas crawled in and settled beside Homer. The partner was skinny, bleached, sunburnt, scraggle-bearded, and worn down from the brutal mucking and digging. He had been a cooper in Ohio once. The perfection that he once brought to his trade, making watertight flawless kegs, he brought to his mining. No man on the bar got as much color out of a panful of gravel. That was one of many reasons Homer considered himself lucky in his choice of a partner.

"It ain't fair," Phineas said. "Just ain't the way things are supposed to be."

Homer appreciated the sympathy, but didn't feel like talking.

"Partner, if you're thinking the time's come, you've got to make some decisions," Phineas said.

"Leave me be, now, Phin."

"I won't. This is the time. It's come up now, and you've got to wrestle with it. You're clear-headed and you can give me some answers."

Resignedly, Homer listened. He didn't want to deal with death.

"You've got a jar full of gold there. What do you want done with it?"

"I don't know."

"Well, should we send it to your family? We can get it cashed out in San Francisco and send a draft."

Homer had two married sisters and a mother scattered through western Indiana. They could all use the money, though none was hurting. He didn't want them to know he was dying. They'd all opposed him. He came anyway, getting up a small outfit consisting of a mule and packsaddle off his mother's farm. It turned out to be the best way to come. He had walked to California, leading the mule, arriving with the vanguard, well ahead of most of the overland Forty-Niners, with the mule in good shape. He had sold the valuable beast for a tent and gear and grub.

"I'll think about it," he said, wishing he didn't have to.

"No, I'm wanting an answer now."

That irritated Homer and he slid into melancholia that closed out the world. What earthly difference did anything make?

Phineas stared a while, his lips forming and rejecting words. "You're not acting like the old Homer Winslow I partnered up with," he said softly. "It's important how a man checks out. You can quit or you can go in style. You haven't much choice, I'll confess that. But a fellow can put up a good show of it."

Homer wished the man would back out of the tent and fix his supper, but Phin had some sort of itch and was going to babble on.

"I'm thirsty," Homer said.

Phin slipped away and returned with a tin cup full of icy water. He helped Homer sip. Not that it did any good. Homer was always thirsty, and not a drop stayed in him.

"Well, Homer, are you glad you came?" Phin asked.

"Yes."

It had been the great adventure of his young life. He hadn't considered himself reckless, though others thought that anyone crazy enough to cross a continent on foot was reckless. He'd defied his family — hurt his ma, who had to hire a man to plow her fields. And he was going to die here, but he didn't regret coming. He'd seen things he hardly knew existed. He'd seen wild Indians, Sioux and Pawnee. He'd seen vast herds of black buffalo. He'd seen mountains with a load of snow on top, right in summer. He'd seen mountain men wearing fringed leather, carrying big percussion lock rifles with octagonal barrels and talking a peculiar tongue. He'd been scared by a grizzly with two cubs, had a prairie rattler crawl right over his bedroll, chased off a red varmint trying to steal his good mule and almost got clubbed doing it. He reckoned he'd stuffed most of a regular lifetime into the past ten months, and that made dying a little easier. He'd done it all on his own, against the entreaties of his ma and Sara and Josephine, too, and that made him right proud, as if he'd cut loose and come up a man.

But if it made dying easier, it didn't make it any better. He'd sparked Melissa a few times back on the farm. Melissa lived two farms over and across the creek, which he negotiated by walking over a fallen tree. She was Abe Stowell's youngest, but it hadn't come to anything, and now he was dying without ever knowing a woman or having a wife or having a child, and that knocked his spirits into the dirt whenever he thought of it. Nothing about dying was more of a cheat than that.

"Yes, I'm glad I came," he said. "No regrets about coming here. I did a lot of living."

"It took something to come, I'll say that. Lots of people didn't. Some didn't even believe the news, even after the government in Washington announced it. Some came. I came. A mess are sailing around the Horn, or crawling across Panama right now. They'll be here. Seems to me a fellow who's done all that, grubbed out well over two thousand and still has nine hundred in good dust after paying the freight...well, it seems to me a fellow like that should do some mighty good dying."

It irked Homer. "I'm the one not going to see anything any more, not you, so button your lips."

Phin retreated but wouldn't let go of it. "I'm sorry, Homer. You have any thoughts about the hereafter? You want us to fetch a preacher? There's a dozen on the bars, to hear tell of it. We'll ask around."

"Oh, I don't know. I never did figure it all out, Phin. I've tried to live up to what was expected of me and be a decent fellow. I guess it's like trust. I'll just trust that if there's something good waiting for my soul, it'll be there for me."

"You want me to fetch a preacher and say some words when the time comes?"

Phin wasn't going to let go of it. Homer could see that. Well, maybe there was some good in it. Even this talk had wearied him so much he felt pure cold death crawling up his limbs. "Don't look special for one, but if one's handy it's all right. It's mostly for you, not for me. What a preacher does is give heart to the living, and that's fine with me. I won't be hearing it."

"All right," said Phin. "Now, tell me who to write in Indiana. You've got folks there. I'll send word. I promise I will, with the next man leaving the bar for Sacramento."

Something stirred in Homer. Memories flooded back on him. "Phin, when I croak, don't you say one word. Don't you write them. Just bury me proper."

"Homer, they're your kin."

"You listen to me. This is what I want, and a dying man ought to get what he wants!"

Phin was plainly puzzled.

Homer was remembering some bad moments back there in Greene County, moments that irked him then and enraged him now. "Listen," he said urgently. "When I let 'em know back there that I was going to head West and make my fortune, I never heard the like. It wasn't just Ma and my sisters, though they were bad enough. Everyone in the county! Like Abe Stowell. He had eighty acres and some dairy cows and I was sweet on his girl. I told old Abe what I was fixing to do, and he got sort of stern and thunder-cloudy, and I could feel the wind coming up and the rain start landing on me. He said... Don't go. It would all come to nothing. There was too much risk. I was chasing moonbeams. A fellow running across a continent full of wild Injuns wasn't the type to make a good husband.

"That was just the start. The grocer, he told me it was folly. Said I'd come to nothing and take sick and go broke. Said it wouldn't profit me. And Missus Hope, she was the minister's wife. She said it was all wrong, I'd fall into evil, and all that. The truth of it, Phin, was that I stood alone and left alone. There wasn't a man or woman or girl or fellow that ever gave me a blessing or said that I was doing something pretty fine, pretty special, pretty daring, pretty smart, pretty courageous! They all saw what was wrong with it, and not a one saw what was right. By the time I'd heard the whole lot, I felt like telling them they didn't know what this big new land was for. It's for making dreams come true. It's for risking and trying and making it. But they'd gotten all narrowed down, trying to make a good life out of avoiding trouble or challenge. So I just took off. I said to myself, they don't know how to live! You following me?"

"You're making mighty good sense. Half the men on this bar had to wrestle with skeptics and naysayers. Most won't get rich here, but not a one regrets coming and trying, and even if they take only memories out of here, they'll make better lives out of what they've been given, just because they came, Homer."

Homer liked that. His partner had it right. "Phin, don't let all those folks back there know. Don't let 'em think they were right. After I go, you just tell people I was a big success and no one's seen me for a while."

"I'll do that, Homer. You're a success. You made a good claim, took thousands out, and everyone admired you."

"That's right, and you tell every fellow on Mad Mule Bar that's how I want it. My folks, they'll find out I croaked eventually, mostly because they lost contact. But don't you tell 'em. If my ghost has to hear all those I-Told-You-Sos, I'll come and haunt you!" Homer laughed. He hadn't laughed in weeks. It hurt his body.

Phineas did too, with a strange tenderness. "It's a promise. And I'll make every man here promise it. Now, Homer, what about that dust?"

Something almost feverish seemed to grip Homer. "I want a little celebration, a little hurrah. That's over five pounds of dust. It'll buy me a big hurrah. I want a good box, and I don't care about the cost. There's mahogany and teak coming into the bay, and everything else. Find a cabinetmaker and make me a good box. I want a fancy one, and I want a parade somewhere. Maybe after winter closes in. I want all my friends on this bar to make a parade, right through Sacramento City, carrying that mighty fine box, and I want you to tell 'em I grubbed a lot of gold and I wanted to check out in style, and there I am. And after that, you pick out a good saloon and set up drinks with that dust until it's gone. And when they ask who I am, you tell 'em I came West and I found gold and I did what I set out to do, and no one can argue it."

"Ah, Homer, that's a good plan," said Phin softly. "Count on me. I won't let you down."

Excitement coursed through Homer. All this seemed impossibly important. "Now, Phin, there's something else. You remember that week we took off because it was so hot a man couldn't pan gold except for a couple hours after dawn? We took off. We put our tools on the claims to hold them a bit, and we got a ride to Stockton with that freight outfit. And we went to that fandango."

"I remember, Homer."

"Phin, I'd hardly set eyes on a woman for months, and there were those *señoritas*, nice girls, daughters of all those *hacendados* around there, and they let us in and let us do some fandangoing. Well, Phin, I danced with the prettiest lady I've ever laid eyes on, golden and laughing with shining eyes and her feet patting around so fast I couldn't keep up. Do you remember her?"

"Sort of."

"Well, her name was Margarita." Homer hesitated, collecting his thoughts. "This is awful hard on you, Phin, and say no if you don't want to. I'd like a lock of her hair going into the box with me. Maybe she won't remember me. Maybe you'll need another lock. Just some shiny black hair, and don't tell my ghost about the switch."

"What was her surname, Homer?"

"Blamed if I know. Just Margarita."

"I'll try, Homer."

Homer sighed. "It's important. Dying's hard when you haven't sampled all of life. I've never gotten hitched up, and I never had me a child, and I never woke up in the morning to find some sweet Margarita beside me, sleepy, trusting, smiling, awaiting a hug and a smile from me. On that account, I don't like this dying at all. But, Phineas, just put a lock of a lady's hair in with me. Wherever I'm going, I'll take it up there and tell the boss I got shortchanged a little and I want to take this in there."

Phin turned aside and hid his face in deep shadow. The light out there was fading fast.

"You go fix your supper, Phin," Homer said. "Now you've got the whole plan."

"I have the whole plan, Homer," Phin said, sliding out.

"I don't want anything," Homer said.

"But you've got to eat. And the broth helps a little."

"Not any more," Homer said.

He lay back, sensing that life was fleeing him, and he wouldn't see the dawn. But it was all right. Thanks to Phineas he had done his accounting and found he'd made a profit. He might have hung on for a day or two or three, but he didn't need to any more.

"It's been mighty fine," he said, feeling the night come.

LOOKING FOR LOVE
AT A ROMANCE
WRITERS CONVENTION

It was the best idea I ever had. And I still think so, even though I got educated pretty fast, and learned stuff I never knew about women. But before I get into all that, I have some explaining to do.

My name is Randy Ransom, and I make my living writing Westerns. I don't sell a whole lot, and I have to keep scrambling, but my publishers pop those pocketbooks into the racks wherever Louis L'Amour doesn't command a pocket, and I make my wages out of it. You've seen plenty of my books, even if you don't read Westerns. They get spread around pretty well.

I'm a forty-two-year-old bachelor, reasonably presentable if you don't look too close at the jug ears and bald spot and lumpy nose, but I figure that doesn't matter so much. When I get dressed up I make sure there's a crease in my Levi's. I'm trim and athletic-looking, and keep my boots polished, except for the pair I wear when I'm mucking around in the corrals.

I've got a dandy little spread on the Big Horn River south of Worland, Wyoming. It's nestled into the bottoms along the river, and there's some good pasture in there for my roan quarter horses. My house started as a double-wide, but I've added onto it, so now there's a nice shady porch, a new office with bay windows overlooking the shimmering river, and a big Earth Stove in one corner that helps me heat up the place on cold days. It's sort of an Eden, you see. Half a section of green grass and some good timber, and any time I saddle up I can head out into the sagebrush-covered hills around there, and ride one of my good saddlers for miles without even coming up against a fence. And I have to tell you, a good spread like that has been the inspiration of a lot of my stories.

I was married once about the time high school got tiresome, and that was all right for a while. I liked marriage, even if Patsy thought it was some sort of indentured servitude. I hustled a journalism degree from the university at Laramie, and spent a bunch of years on small papers around the state, so I knew how to write obituaries and church socials. I advanced from places like Rock Springs and Rawlins and Thermopolis to Jackson and then to Casper, which is a big up-scale metropolitan outfit that even puts out a Sunday edition. Somewhere along in there, Patsy cut the strings, and I was on my own.

Casper's a petroleum town, and it rides up and down with the price of oil. I was doing just fine until one of those oil gluts knocked the props out of the local economy, and before I knew it, I'd been laid off, and suddenly things looked a little bleak. But that was after eleven years of toil on the city desk, and I'd put aside a bit. Enough to buy me some land and live the way I always wanted, provided that I could sell what I wrote.

So that's how come I got to own some good river-bottom land in rural Wyoming, and how come I churn out those pocketbooks with cowboys on the covers, three a year, as regular as a metronome. I had a knack, and now I'm pretty secure, and there are readers out there who pluck up every book of mine they see.

The only trouble with all this is that living in the country is pretty lonesome. There I was, with a piece of the West, some obedient geldings and a few dogs, doing what I loved doing. I was free of all bosses and corporations, enjoying my library, my office, my sunrise view of the river and the mule deer along it, the antelope up on the sagebrush hills, the Canada geese, my round corral, the good roan quarter horses I raised, the smell of new-baled alfalfa, the joy I took in shoeing my own horses, and it was all fine — except I was almighty lonesome. I kept thinking I needed just one more thing, and that was a wife who loved the West, too, loved to ride, loved the wild open land, loved the red willows and the elk along the river, loved Doc Holliday and Wyatt Earp and Crazy Horse and the Old West and the fine traditions of ranching people, and enjoyed gabbing with authors.... Well, I guess you can see where this is drifting.

I live a few miles south of Worland, so that's where I go when I want company. There's some mighty fine people there, and I often wander into the Washakie Hotel's soft-lit bar and settle down for some good times. I'm sort of a local celebrity, being a writer, and half the time the Coors come free, and once in a while I even scrawl my John Henry over the title page of one of those little paperbacks with cowboys on the cover.

But I mostly go there to talk about quarter horses and elk hunting, which is what people do around there. I have kept an eye on the gals for years, and there's some nice trim single ones who wander in there — good-looking teachers and social workers and one who makes hamburger in the Safeway meat department — but somehow I never much took to them, or maybe they never quite took to me, not knowing what to make of a writer, and so our conversations always fizzle out in elaborate pleasantness, and things don't progress beyond a movie or renting a video tape or going out for an eight-ounce rib-eye steak, medium well.

This was pretty serious business. There were times that I got my hopes up, and began dreaming of a nest for two, but somehow they fizzled out. Especially in the winters, when there wasn't much to do outside, I would start to ache. I'd remember all my sweethearts — there weren't very many — and just ache. Christmases were awful. My life wasn't complete. There was a big hole right in the middle of it. I did come close once, with a sweet twenty-three-year old blonde with some kind of certificate that made her a veterinarian's assistant, so we had horses in common, and she could geld a stud colt so fast it made me quake, but one day she sent me a bouquet of lavender irises and a nice note that said she had found someone else. Horsing around with someone else, that's what I thought. No gal in the middle of Wyoming dreams of hitching up with a writer.

But I do have a writing buddy in the area, and I sometimes get together with her when I want to talk books and agents, and how publishers screw authors, and all of that. Her name is Maggie Yurovich, and she writes those women's romances under the name of Connie Woo. Her romances all feature a ninety-pound Chinese or Korean gal who's a black belt in Karate or Taekwondo, and these heroines get rid of unwanted two hundred-pound male attention with a good chop or a kick of their dainty feet, until the right guy comes along and they fall in love and marry him instead of kicking him in the crotch. How Maggie got into that I'll never know, but she sells romances by the bucketful, and makes about ten times what I do, and keeps telling me to quit writing horse opera and start making a few bucks.

"Randy, what you should do is come to one of the romance writers conventions and get with it," she said. "Don't be so negative. There are some guys that write them. They use a woman's name. Like Rachel Ransom."

Well, hell.

Maggie's divorced, and has a steady guy, and a couple of pimpled teen-aged kids, and is happy in her life, so I have no romantic feeling toward her. But we're the only writers in a fifty-mile radius, and we get together for lunch at Granny's Café or maybe just black coffee now and then to talk shop, and I enjoy her company. I don't know where she learned all that about love, but she knows the field and never has any trouble selling her stuff to Harlequin or Silhouette, and those Connie Woo books plaster the racks in some places, especially Amarillo and San Diego and Little Rock.

I guess knowing Maggie is where the big idea came from.

I'd sure gotten frustrated trying to find a mate around Worland, Wyoming. Writers live pretty solitary lives, and that worked against it. I wasn't out in the bustling world, slaving away for some big company, meeting new people every day.

Worland wasn't much of a literary center, either, and the gals I did meet just couldn't talk books with me, and most couldn't even talk Western history with me. They'd never heard of Crazy Horse for crying out loud, and there just wasn't enough to bridge the gap between them and me. So I wasn't getting anywhere. I had to do something.

Like go to a romance writers convention. They have an outfit, just the way most genre fiction writers have an outfit. The Western writers go to their convention, and the mystery writers go to theirs, and the romance writers go to theirs. Romances sell better than anything else, so the publishers and editors swarm to the romance conventions, and throw big shindigs and have fancy hospitality suites, so a guy could pretty well stuff himself at one of those conventions and never even have to buy breakfast. It wouldn't cost a whole lot. That's what Maggie said.

But that wasn't really what interested me. Maggie told me that a thousand female writers show up at one of those shindigs, attending seminars and panels about love and writing and romance. That's a lot of female writers. I found out later about a dozen guys show up, too, mostly spouses. Every one of those gals would be a connoisseur of love, and men, and writing. And plenty would be single. You could hardly be a romance writer and be married. I mean, how could they do research? I liked the idea. There'd be stuff to talk about. Things in common.

Well, the more I thought about it, the better it got. I was as good as married. I would add another office to the double wide, and hook it all together into a sprawling ranch house, and my beloved and I would write our books, and go for horseback rides, and evening strolls along the river, and sit before my crackling wood stove on a winter's evening and hug each other. I'd encourage her when she was blue, help her if she needed help, hug her when she needed a hug, and make her life beautiful any way I could. Ah, the more I contemplated it, the better it all seemed. I began to feel downright perky with that idea bucking around in me.

Of course, I corralled Maggie to talk about this. I was a little guarded; I didn't quite want her to know I was going to go to the romance writers convention to find a mate. But I did pepper her with lots of questions, and she agreed that if I went to the next one, at the Sheraton in Seattle, she'd introduce me around and I could get some idea what the romance business was all about. So that's how come one August day I loaded my gear into my new white Chevy pickup truck, turned on the air conditioning, and drove west.

Heading for the romance writers convention just plain fueled me with dreams. As that truck sailed through Idaho and Oregon and into Washington, I just knew I was getting close to the best thing that ever happened to me. I'd find my bride, all right. She'd be slim and pretty and warm. She'd know all about books and writing. She'd be supportive and affectionate. She'd love the West. Of course I would have to be flexible, and see the merits in these gals, and adjust a little here and there. But I felt sort of like a miner who had hit a bonanza. A thousand women, and hardly another male in sight! Why, the idea was so dazzling I marveled that no other guy had thought it up before. One guy and a thousand eager women! I was almost feeling smug about it.

Seattle is a toney place, and the Sheraton was big, white, and fancy, and when I pulled into the parking garage, I could see at once that my pickup didn't belong. I parked between a BMW and a Lexus, and across from a Lincoln Town Car, pulled my ditty bag out of the truck bed, and headed for the registration desk. Those romance writers made plenty of moolah, and could afford cars like that, and hotels like this. I checked in, got to my room, and thought it was no fancier than some I'd seen in Casper or Cheyenne. I had a bad moment then, that I'm embarrassed to tell about. I saw that other bed and wished some sweetheart were claiming it, and for a moment I felt blue. But I perked up fast. That's just what I had come to the romance writers convention for, wasn't it?

I cleaned up and put on my good Palm Beach gray tweed sport coat, with the leather patches at the elbow. That over a blue oxford cloth shirt and jeans and Nocona boots made an odd combination, but I figured that's who I was, and it was too late to become something else.

Then I hopped the elevator down to the mezzanine, where the action was, and was smacked with a wall of noise the moment I stepped out. The place was full of women, and all of them were gabbing. I kept an eye out for Maggie, but I really didn't want to see her just then. I wanted to sort of case the joint, get some idea of what a convention of romance writers looked and smelled like.

So I sort of sidled around that big reception area, surveying all these ladies who were collected into knots and jabbering. I had expected a lot of perfume in the air, but there was very little.

What struck me, and I'll always remember this, was that about half the women wore a sort of uniform that consisted of a muumuu and sandals and horn rimmed glasses. That wasn't what I expected romance writers to look like. At first I couldn't even remember the name of those gaudy Polynesian dresses that hung from the shoulders in great diaphanous folds, and had no waists, but muumuu came to mind. There was enough fabric in any one of those to make a two-man tent. Of course some women dressed in other ways, but the muumuu crowd dominated. Most of them had painted their toenails red or pink, and in the space of a few minutes I saw more painted toenails than I would expect to see around a hundred Vegas swimming pools.

The other women mostly wore skirts, blouses, and blazers. I could see in a glance at their left hands that most of these were married, but I had expected that. Even before coming to Seattle, I had calculated that if I found a hundred single women out of the thousand, I would be doing well. The muumuu ladies were harder to fathom because they had so many rings on so many fingers I couldn't make much sense of their marital status, unless they were all polygamists.

I have to confess that all those gals in muumuus weren't what I was looking for, even though I was trying hard to be open-minded. I just couldn't imagine one of them wandering around my ranch house in one of those technicolor tents, stubbing her toes on my furniture and peering at me from soft, pouty eyes behind horn-rimmed glasses. I could sort of see why they were so interested in writing romance fantasies that might appeal to trapped housewives.

So, within minutes of my arrival, I had already eliminated half the romance writers. But that didn't discourage me at all. In fact, it helped. But as I looked around that mezzanine full of gabbing, hurrying women, I felt a little lost. I didn't know any of them, and finding a sweetheart was going to be a lot harder than I thought it would be back there in the safety of my dreams in Wyoming. I was the only male on the mezzanine, and that made things worse, not better.

I strolled over to the message boards so I could see what was what, the panels and seminars and all that. There sure would be a mess of them: I could choose to hear about Publishing Contracts, Libel and Privacy Law, The Spiritual in Romance Writing, Male Code Words, Female Code Words, Coming On to the One You Want, Marketing the Romance, Teen-Age Romance, Senior Romance, New Divorcées Romance, First Love, Romance Mysteries, Romance Westerns, The *Ménage à Trois*, Romance Science Fiction, The Myth of Love-Hungry Widows, Romance True Crime, Diseases of the Heart and Soul, Romeo and Juliet: Romantic Suicide, Ghosts, Goblins, Were-wolves, and Love, D.H. Lawrence and the Romantic Mésalliance, Romance Horror, Death Row Marriage and Romance, What We Learned from Frederick's of Hollywood, Love on Bad Hair Days, Romance for Swinging Singles, Trailer Park Romances, The Ins and Outs of Motel Rendezvous, Imaginative Honeymoons, Tropical

Paradises, Multicultural Romance, Love Among the Inhibited, It Takes More Than Victoria's Secret, and a whole lot more. I thought I would sample the trailer park romance, but first I'd go find out where all those fancy hospitality suites were located, and maybe munch grapes and pineapple off Bantam or Berkley.

That's when Maggie zeroed in.

"Hey, you made it! A familiar face! What do you think?"

"Aren't there any men?"

"A few. Mostly editors. You'll get used to it. You want to meet people?"

"Sure."

"How about if I just point a few out? There's a lot of success and money floating around here."

She took hold of my elbow and steered me into the female sea. "See that gal there, with the blue hair? She's Monette Spruille, and she earns half a million a year on bad years. See that little granny there? That's Meg V. Mercer, and she's parlayed a series about love triangles and mate swapping in upper Manhattan into a million bucks. See that slim little thing with the pony tail? She writes love stories with plain heroines, you know, flat-chested and receding chins, and they sell by the millions, can't keep 'em in the warehouses, out the door. Biggest thing in romance. Now she's got a whole line of new ones about wheel-chair love, and she's starting one about plastic surgery and love, and next is going to be post-chemo love, no hair and all that. Sandy Augusta Prill, that's her name. You ought to talk with her. She's subcontracting the stories out. You could be maybe Becky Randolph on the cover and earn ten thousand a crack."

"I'm not ready to be a Becky, Maggie."

She eyed me coldly. "This is business. You do what you have to do or starve."

She steered me down a long hall toward the meeting rooms, and then whooped.

"Hey, there's someone you should meet. Lindy!"

A lovely, slim, fortyish chestnut-haired woman with a piquant smile on her lips hugged Maggie and they fussed over each other for a moment.

"Randy, this is Lindy Q. Lawton. She writes for Harlequin," Maggie said. "And this is my friend Randy Ransom."

Lindy looked at me so warmly that I felt aglow. Here was the woman! And I had hardly started looking!

"I'm so pleased to meet you at last," Lindy said. "I've heard a little about you."

"You have?"

"Of course. Now who are you with?"

"Ah, Fawcett and Warner."

"That's odd, two companies. Are they all part of one conglomerate, or am I missing something?"

"Nope, separate companies all right. But I've been with both for years."

She laughed. "I'll never figure it out," she said. "Tell me about yourself."

"Well, I live in Wyoming, have a great little spread, raise quarter horses, and love the West."

"Oh, they let you do that? I've heard that's the new thing. Fax, modems, FedEx, it doesn't matter where you work." She smiled. "It sounds like a good life."

I sure liked this gal, and she liked me. I could see that. "It's an idyll," I said.

"Say, could we talk business?" she asked. "I'd like to ask your advice."

"You two talk. I'm going to take in the panel on marketing," Maggie said.

Next thing I knew, Lindy was leading me back to the mezzanine to a group of stuffed chairs, and I could tell by her smiles that I was a pretty popular fellow. I guess the feeling was mutual. I liked her voice, her smiles, her easy walk, the nice blue blazer she wore, and the soft way she did her chestnut hair, and the glow in her face.

"Can I get you some coffee or something?" I asked.

"Oh, no, I just want some advice. You see, Harlequin isn't giving me the advances that I should be getting based on my numbers, and I'm thinking about switching."

"Well, I'm not sure I'm the one to talk to."

She patted my hand. "Of course you are, Randy. I'm thinking I ought to be demanding fifty thousand advances, but it's sort of scary, demanding that. And my agent...Sharon Schwartz...she's against it. What do you think?"

"Well, ah, I'm really not one to say."

She grinned. "Professional courtesy. You're with other companies. Well, O.K. Would you read a manuscript? I would just love to switch to Warner, and I would love to have you take over my career...."

I finally understood. "Lindy, I'm not an editor."

She stared, bewildered. "You're not? But I thought...."

"I'm a writer."

"Oh...romances?"

"Westerns."

She laughed. "I sure was confused. I thought Maggie was introducing me to an editor. She said she would." She sighed. "I would have loved to do business."

"Are you free for dinner, Lindy? I'd sure enjoy getting to know you."

"Oh, no, I'm sorry. Other plans."

"How about coffee right now?"

"No, I appreciate the offer but...."

"I was going to head for the Harlequin hospitality suite up on the top floor. Want to go up? You could show me some of your books."

She shook her head, and stood. "Mister Ransom, there are so many panels that I need to attend. It's been so nice...."

Lindy Q. Lawton vanished down a corridor. I began to see how the love business is.

I caught an elevator to the penthouse floor, and entered a suite bedecked with Harlequin posters, a literature table, heaps of free pocketbooks, and a lengthy trestle table groaning with fruits, beverages, sweets, finger food, sandwiches, juices, salads, and desserts. No wonder the romance writers wore muumuus.

I grazed my way through the heaped food, knowing I wouldn't have to eat again for a week. I spotted a nice, slim redhead in a hot pink pant suit rummaging through the free books, so I maneuvered around to get a look at her ring finger and found it empty. A good sign.

She wore a name tag, but I couldn't see who she was. But that was all right. I'm not shy.

"Hi. I'm Randy," I said.

She turned to face me, and her glance sufficed to read all the vital statistics. "I don't doubt it," she replied.

I was off to a bad start. "Randolph Ransom," I said. "And you?"

"Missus John Dillard. I work for Harlequin Toronto."

Well, that's how the day went.

I wandered into one of the panel discussion rooms, and discovered a standing-room-only crowd, so I hunched against a wall. The speaker was a solemn gray-haired woman with gold-rimmed granny glasses, and marketing was her topic.

"It breaks down this way," she was saying. "In eighteen percent of romance novels, the heroine makes love and enjoys every moment of it. In twenty-seven percent, the heroine gets physical but feels guilty about it, especially if she does it with more than one hero. This category, by the way, oddly enough, commands the biggest advances...the average contract is for forty-seven thousand dollars. The next category, which commands thirty-one percent of the market, has the heroine not getting into bed, but wishing desperately she could. This is a very popular category, and housewives really empathize, but the advances are lower because there is so much competition out there. Figure on getting only twenty-five thousand for a novel in this category.

"And of course the remaining category is for heroines who don't climb into bed and don't want to do it until they get married, popular among teen girls and in the religious romance market, and this commands seventeen percent of the market, and also the advances are quite low, usually seven to ten thousand. Now that doesn't add up to a hundred percent, because there are some odd fringe categories. But as a rule, I'd say to maximize your profits, write romances in which the heroine does it but feels guilty, or doesn't do it but wants to.

"Now, there is another important datum. There is a direct correlation between sales, advances, and the frequency of encounters per book. The best numbers, often ranging from fifty thousand on up to a million in sales, are for novels in which the heroine makes love five to seven times. When the heroine does it only once or twice, the sales fall sharply, even though this is for some readers the most moving and exciting type of romance. Anything below four point three physical encounters and you will be losing money. Some of you will prefer to work in this category, but you'll do it at some financial sacrifice. I myself prefer this sort of story because it builds better when the heroine finally does it at the end of the story. There is also a successful variant in which the heroine tries it once with someone she doesn't like, regrets it, and then waits for her true heart to come along and tries it again at the end of the story and really likes it.

"Now here's another surprise. Our research shows that readers much prefer stories in which the heroine is the initiator. Seventy-two percent of readers prefer that the heroine take the initiative, while twenty percent prefer that the hero take the initiative, and the result is reflected in sales and advances. We think it has to do with women taking command of their lives. If you want to maximize your romance sales and profits, then have a seductive heroine who initiates five to seven encounters but is a little guilty about them. I'd say that if you do this consistently, you will earn advances of eighty-five to two hundred thousand per novel."

I thought that was pretty interesting. At least I would know what sold best, if I ever decided to write romances. The romance writers were listening raptly, and taking copious notes.

That afternoon I attended a panel on romance covers, and learned that the best ones featured a bare-chested male model, one of several famous ones with single names and long hair, while the pictured heroine had plenty of bosom and wild hair. But, paradoxically, the second most successful cover category had no human images at all, but featured hearts and flowers and vines and other simple symbols of love. The women were listening attentively, and, after the panel was done, peppered the panelists with questions about how they could persuade their publishers to do different covers. As one pointed out from the floor, a good cover was the difference between a half-million-dollar seller, and one that didn't even make the charts, and she'd be damned if she would put up with crummy covers any more.

By late afternoon I was out of sorts, having had more than my fill of love, so I repaired to the quiet Sheraton Hotel bar, and there discovered all twelve of the males attending the convention. They were spouses, and had learned to spend a romance writers convention in the saloon with others in similar distress. I nodded cheerfully, ordered a Coors, and settled in for some good times.

THE END

ABOUT THE AUTHOR

Richard S. Wheeler, born in Milwaukee, Wisconsin, emerged as an author of the Western story at the age of forty-three with BUSHWACK (1978), followed by the highly praised BENEATH THE BLUE MOUNTAIN (1979). Already this early work was characterized by off-trail storylines, avoidance of any appeal to myth or legendry, and a rejection of upbeat resolutions. Following a hiatus of a few years in which he published nothing, Wheeler brought out what remains his masterpiece, WINTER GRASS (1983). It was finalist that year for the Spur Award from the Western Writers of America. It was, however, his later novel, FOOL'S COACH (1989), that earned him his first Spur Award. His more recent work, such as CASHBOX (1994) and GOLDFIELD (1995), has been more ambitious, taking a wider spectrum of history into account in narrating the complex lives of his characters set against distinctive historical backgrounds. The period between 1989 and 1993 was an extraordinarily productive one for Wheeler during which he published no less than eighteen novels and averaged 250,000 words a year. He also deserves recognition for his special talent as an editor — for eight years he worked for Walker and Company for their Westerns line and brought a number of notable writers to the fore by recommending their first novels for publication.